C

MW01193938

A Chocolate Centered Cozy Mystery Series

Cindy Bell

Copyright © 2017 Cindy Bell
All rights reserved.

ISBN-13: 978-1545308783

ISBN-10: 1545308780

Table of Contents

Chapter One

A smooth stream of melted chocolate poured into the heart mold. Ally watched the way it folded and pooled. Something about the way that chocolate poured so gracefully always relaxed her.

"Ally? Do you have the piping bag so I can write the initials on?"

"Yes, I do."

"I'll start piping the decorations later. Can you make sure you make some white chocolates, too, the bride and groom requested both."

"Okay." Ally grabbed some white chocolate and began to melt it to add to the mold. "I think this is such a clever thing to have as a keepsake from the wedding."

"Yes, it won't last long though." Charlotte grinned as she slid a mold into the refrigerator. "Not as delicious as these will be."

"No, but the memory will. We should add

these to our wedding menu, I think it would be a very popular choice."

"You're right we should. I'm sure you would enjoy having it at your wedding."

"My wedding?" Ally laughed. "That day is already long gone." She poured the white chocolate into the remaining molds.

"Well, the first one." Charlotte shrugged.

"The last one." Ally pursed her lips, then slid the mold into the refrigerator. "At least, for now."

"Well, that for now gives me hope." Charlotte smiled. She leaned back against the counter beside her granddaughter. "Life is too sweet to ever let yourself get bitter, Ally."

"I know, I know." Ally looked over at her with a half-smile. "How can I be bitter with an amazing man like Luke in my life?"

"Good point." Charlotte grinned.

"And I'm not the only one. When am I going to have a chance to meet the man in your life?"

"I wouldn't call him the man in my life. He's a

man, that's a friend."

"Yes, I've heard this story before. But it doesn't change the glint in your eye when you talk about him." Ally shot her grandmother a knowing smile. "I'd love the chance to meet him."

"And you'll have it, soon enough."

"Really?"

"Sure." Charlotte cleared her throat.

"You're avoiding, aren't you? Are you afraid that I'll scare him away?" Ally frowned. "I'll be nice, I promise."

"Oh, Ally it's not that at all." Charlotte hugged her with a firm squeeze. "It's just that I like things with him the way they are. Things are relaxed and he is a nice companion, it's nothing serious."

"I can understand that. But honestly, I don't think you have anything to worry about. I plan to greet him at the door with a shotgun and warn him not to hurt you, that's all."

"Ha ha." Charlotte grinned as she grabbed some more chocolate to melt. "No, I do want you to meet him. I know that he wants to meet you and he keeps asking about spending some time with you, which I think is sweet. You know what, let's have dinner tomorrow night."

"Yes! I'm so excited."

"And bring Luke, it'll be good for everyone to get to know each other better."

"That sounds perfect. He makes costume jewelry, right?" Ally walked over to the sink to wash her hands. "The pieces you have are beautiful."

"Yes, he's quite talented, he also makes custom-made pieces. Did you make the white chocolate roses yet?"

"Yes, I'm getting ready to package them up." Ally dried her hands, then slipped on some gloves. As she began to pop the roses out of the molds she smiled. "They came out perfect."

"Great." Charlotte breathed a sigh of relief. "I get so nervous about weddings. It's such a big day."

"I don't know, I don't think marriage is that big of a deal."

"You don't?"

Ally jumped at the sound of the familiar voice. "Luke? I didn't even hear you come in." She turned around to face him, her cheeks hot.

"The back door was open." He peered past her at the chocolate. "Wow, those look delicious. Now what were you saying about..."

"Here try one." Ally popped a chocolate rose in his mouth. He gulped with surprise, then closed his eyes as the chocolate melted on his tongue.

"Mm." He sighed, then wrapped his arms around her.

"Nice save." Charlotte mouthed to Ally over Luke's shoulder.

Ally buried her lips in Luke's shoulder to hide her grin. When she pulled away from the hug he gave her a quick kiss.

"Sweet, but not as sweet as you."

"Aw." Ally winked at him. "I bet you say that

to all the chocolate-makers."

"Nope, just you."

"It's almost time to open." Charlotte glanced at the wooden clock on the wall. "I'll go out front and make sure that everything is in place. Ally, can you finish up these hearts please? I have almost finished the milk chocolate ones."

"Sure." Ally took over stirring the chocolate as it melted. Once they were alone, Luke stepped closer to her.

"So, about what you were saying..."

"I don't know what you mean." She stirred faster.

"Relax, I'm just teasing you." He laughed and kissed her cheek.

"You're so mean." She sighed. "Oh, before I forget, Mee-Maw invited us to dinner with Jeffrey tomorrow night. Do you think you'll be able to make it?"

"Sure, I'm off tomorrow afternoon."

"Oh, that's right. Any plans?"

"I might take a drive over to Freely to look at wedding venues. Because you know how important that is to me."

"Stop it!" She gave him a swat on his stomach. He caught her hand and pulled her close.

"I might just decide to see if I can steal you away from Charlotte's Chocolate Heaven and take you for a long drive through the country."

"Oh, that sounds wonderful."

"Yes, especially if you bring the left-over chocolates." He raised an eyebrow.

"I think that can be arranged." She laughed. "It's a short opening day tomorrow, but I need to be here in the morning. Mee-Maw is going to deliver the chocolates to the wedding. After that, I'm all yours."

"I guess I can wait that long, if I must."

"Here." She popped another chocolate into his mouth. "That should hold you over."

"Yum!" He stole a quick kiss before she went back to work. Ally couldn't help but blush. As she watched him walk away, she reminded herself of just how lucky she was. The more time she spent with Luke the more certain she was that he was an amazing person.

"All clear in here?" Charlotte poked her head into the kitchen.

"Yes, Mee-Maw, the mushy stuff is over."

"Oh, good." She smiled.

"I think the bride and groom are going to love these chocolates."

"I hope so. It may seem like just another day to some people, but in that moment, on that day, it means so much to the couple getting married."

"You're right. I'm glad we can be part of their wonderful memory. Speaking of memories, did you call Jeff, yet?"

"I haven't yet. I'll ask him when I get back to Freely Lakes tonight or tomorrow morning."

"Good." Ally smiled.

They spent the rest of the day going between customers and preparing chocolates for the wedding. There was a buzz of excitement in the shop as even though the wedding was of a young couple from the neighboring town of Mainbry, many of the locals that came in were involved in, or knew about the wedding. The small town of Blue River made everyone's business everyone's business. Sometimes it was a curse, and sometimes it was a comfort.

***

The next morning Charlotte and Ally arrived early at the shop to do the final packaging on the chocolates. Charlotte had purchased special boxes to store them in, and had several three tier trays to set up the rest.

"Do you think everything is just right?" Charlotte paced back and forth in front of the boxes of chocolates. "I don't know why but I feel like we might be missing something."

"It's perfect, Mee-Maw. I've checked and double-checked the order, there's nothing off about it." Ally caught her arm to stop her from pacing. "They are going to be so happy with these."

"Oh good, I'm glad you think so." Charlotte smiled and picked up an extra package. "I also made a big heart with their wedding date on it for them to have as a memento."

"What a great idea!"

"Okay, I guess it's time to load up the van." Charlotte took a deep breath.

"Let's just hope nothing gets dropped."

"Here, I'll help you. We don't have any customers right now."

"Great, the van is already pulled up to the back door." Ally picked up one of the large trays. "Oh, by the way did you confirm dinner with Jeff tonight?"

"Yes, I did. He's all for it. He made a reservation at Moonfield's."

"Oh, fancy." Ally grinned as she carried the tray towards the door.

"I do think he wants to impress you. He is friends with the owner so he was able to get us in."

"Well, consider me impressed." Ally pushed the door open with her elbow and set the tray in the van. Once they had it loaded up, Charlotte headed off for the wedding. Ally was left alone in the shop, a shop that had been like a second home to her since she was a little girl. She loved the delicious smells it contained and the assortment of wooden toys, ornaments, masks, and clocks that decorated the walls. Even though she saw them every day, she always noticed a new detail when she took the time to look.

"Morning Ally!" Mrs. White pushed through the door and announced herself before the bell above the door could even finish its chime. "No time to waste! I have very important meetings to attend!"

"Oh really?" Ally grinned and took the lid off the sample tray. "You might want to try the crushed hazelnut mocha, they are new and delicious."

"Oh yes, thank you." She popped the chocolate into her mouth, then moaned her approval.

"So, what are you so busy with today?" Ally's eyes sparkled as she looked at Mrs. White. She was a fixture of her childhood, and now of her twenties as well. She only occasionally visited the shop alone, she was usually with two of her closest friends. As one of the shop's regulars, she was more like family than a customer.

"There's this grand play in Mainbry, and I am in charge of decorating the sets. It is far more work than I expected. In fact, I'm not so sure I should have signed up for it. But I have, and now I must be the best coordinator I can be."

"I'm sure you will do wonderfully. What kind of play is it?"

"Oh, I have no idea, some old love tragedy or something," she mumbled around another piece of chocolate.

"I thought you said it was grand?" Ally held back a laugh.

"It is grand, the production, the actors, the

rehearsals, did I mention the actors? But the story itself is just another one of those gooey romances. I will never understand the obsession that young people have with love."

"I'm sure it's not just young people. But what do you mean?" She rested her hands on the counter and leaned in to listen.

"In my day, love was about a little more than hormones and blush. It was about companionship, reliability, trust, and good old fashioned common sense. You made a good marriage, and if love came with it fine, but it wasn't the point of the marriage it was just a lovely afterthought."

"Really?" Ally furrowed a brow. "There was that little emotion involved?"

"There were emotions. Like, admiration for each other's abilities, for what the other person brought to the partnership, and a shared interest in your future together."

"I think all of that still exists."

"Maybe, but people don't pay enough attention to it. They want the drama, the pounding hearts, the head over heels nonsense that gets people into trouble."

"Hm, it sounds to me like you might be speaking from experience, Mrs. White."

Her lightly rouged cheeks grew even more pink. "Never mind that, just wrap me up some of these chocolates to go, will you dear?"

"Absolutely." She filled a box with chocolates, then wrapped it up, and rung it up on the register. "I threw in some extra, for the actors." She winked at Mrs. White.

"Oh well, thank you." Mrs. White giggled. "I'm sure they will appreciate it." As she walked out, Luke stepped in.

"Luke, I can't go just yet, Mee-Maw just left for the wedding..."

"Ally." His brows were knitted tight as he walked up to the counter.

"What's wrong?" Her eyes widened. She

didn't often see Luke with such a serious expression, unless he was working a case.

"It's Jeffrey."

"Oh no, has something happened to him?" She gripped the counter to keep herself steady.

"He hasn't been hurt, but something has happened. There was a murder in Broughdon this morning. I checked into it to see if they needed any help with traffic control or knocking on doors, but they already have a suspect."

"What does this have to do with Jeff?" Ally shook her head.

"Jeffrey is the suspect, Ally."

"The suspect?" She stared at him.

"The murder suspect." Luke set his jaw. "Apparently, there is a good amount of evidence against him. He was seen at the scene of the crime a short time before the body was discovered."

"Really? But Mee-Maw thinks he is a nice person. She wouldn't be friends with someone that was violent."

"Some people hide it well." He shrugged.

"Something doesn't make sense here. Can you tell me exactly what happened?"

"According to what I was told, a jewelry shop owner was murdered this morning. Jeffrey was seen leaving the shop right around the time of the murder. He has already been arrested."

"Arrested?" Ally stared at him. "Then they must have some serious evidence."

"I'm not sure what it is yet, all I know is that it had to be enough to put cuffs on him. I'm going to head over and see if I can find out more details. I wanted to tell you first, because I know that Charlotte will be upset about this."

"She will be." Ally grimaced.

"Try not to worry too much. I'll let you know as soon as I find out anything."

"Okay." Ally stared into his eyes. "Do you think it's true? Do you think he did it?"

"Who did what?" Charlotte stepped into the shop through the back door and hung the van keys up behind the counter. "Why are you both staring at me so strangely? Did I do something wrong?"

"I should go." Luke frowned. "I'll update you as soon as I can." He headed for the door.

Chapter Two

Ally faced her grandmother with trepidation. She was unsure of how to tell her that Jeff had been arrested.

"Ally? What's going on?" Charlotte crossed her arms.

"Mee-Maw, there's something I have to tell you. Maybe you should sit down first." Ally gestured to one of the stools at the sample counter.

"I don't need to sit down. Out with it, Ally!" Charlotte locked eyes with her.

"It's Jeff, he's been arrested for murder." Ally spoke the words all in one breath. She didn't know how else to reveal to her grandmother that she was dating a murder suspect.

"What?" Charlotte laughed and waved her hand through the air. "That's ridiculous. Why would you pull a prank like that on me?"

"It's not a prank, Mee-Maw, it's the truth.

He's been arrested for the murder of a jewelry shop owner in Broughdon," Ally said. "Luke is on his way there now to find out what he can. I'm sorry, Mee-Maw, but this is really happening."

"This is ridiculous," Charlotte said. "There must be some mistake. Jeff would never hurt anyone. I know he wouldn't!"

"Maybe you don't think so, Mee-Maw, but they wouldn't have arrested him on a whim. He was spotted at the shop right around the time of the murder. Luke says they have more evidence, he just doesn't know what it is yet."

"No, Ally." She straightened up and stared hard into her granddaughter's eyes. "I'm telling you right now that Jeff didn't have anything to do with this. If he's been arrested, then a terrible mistake has been made, and it needs to be fixed right away." She turned on her heel and headed towards the door. "I'm going there right now to get him out of jail."

"Mee-Maw, wait." Ally grabbed her by the wrist before she could get too far. "It doesn't work like that. The police are going to want to question him first. It's going to take time. If you go there now, you'll just be adding to the chaos. Luke said he'd update me as soon as he finds out anything. It's best if we just stay here for now, all right?"

"I guess you're right." She frowned. "I'm sure all of this will get straightened out very quickly. But poor Jeff, he has to go through all of this, all because of some silly mistake."

"If it's a mistake then I'm sure they will figure it out quickly."

"There's no 'if', Ally. It absolutely is a mistake." She shook her head. "I know Jeff and he is not capable of this. I would not be friendly with a man who was capable of murder."

"I understand." Ally bit into her bottom lip. She wanted to say more, but she wasn't sure how to phrase it. Instead she decided to try and change the subject, to distract them both. "How did the delivery go?"

"What delivery?" Charlotte blinked and her expression grew vacant. "Oh, right. It was fine.

The bride was quite happy, but obviously busy and distracted." She wrung her hands. One foot in front of the other, she began to pace. "When do you think I should go to the jail to see him?"

"It's best to give it a couple of hours at least. But they might be holding him at the police station still."

"Oh, he's going to be so embarrassed, he's such a proud man." Charlotte walked behind the counter and tried to busy herself straightening out the sample trays. "I just can't believe this."

"It's quite a shock. Why don't you let me do that?"

"It's okay, I need to keep myself busy." Charlotte continued to fiddle with the chocolates.

"Mee-Maw, did you notice whether Jeff was upset about anything recently?"

"No, he was looking forward to our dinner tonight. There was nothing wrong." She wiped her hands on a towel, "Maybe you're right, maybe I should find something to do in the back. I don't feel like hearing the customers gossiping about Jeff today."

"We need to make some milk chocolate caramels for an order if you'd like to work on that. Or you could just go home if you want, Mee-Maw, I can handle this."

"No way." Charlotte shook her head. "I'm not going anywhere, except to Jeff."

After Charlotte disappeared into the back, Ally checked her phone. She hoped to hear something from Luke soon. The best news would be that Jeff had been released. However, there were no missed calls or texts. She tried to think of all of the things her grandmother told her about Jeff, in case there were any red flags she'd missed. After some thorough mental digging, she realized she didn't know very much about Jeff at all, and had to wonder if her grandmother really knew as much as she thought she did. Before she could dig any deeper through her thoughts, the bell above the door chimed. She was faced with an entire crowd of people who had just left their Book Club meeting together. As she dealt with the rush, she was relieved not to think about the murder for at least a few minutes. When the last customer left she heard her phone ring. As she reached it, her grandmother popped out of the back room.

"Is it him?" Charlotte stepped close to Ally and peered at her phone.

"Yes, it is. I'll put it on speaker." Ally answered the phone and switched it to speaker so they could both hear. "Hi Luke, you're on speaker."

"Listen, I know it's a short opening day so you are closing soon and I think it's better if we meet to talk about this in person. Is that okay?"

"Yes," Ally said.

"There's a new diner halfway to Broughdon, Lucky's, do you know it?"

"Yes, I know it," Charlotte said. "Jeff and I have met there for lunch."

"Okay, I'll be there in twenty minutes. Just get there when you can."

"We'll be there." Charlotte shook her head as Ally hung up the phone. "That didn't sound very promising."

"One step at a time, Mee-Maw. I'm sure whatever it is, like you said, it will all be straightened out."

"I'll close out the register." Charlotte began to sort through the money in the register. Ally cleaned up all of the samples, the counters, and made sure that everything was off in the kitchen. Once they were ready to leave, Charlotte grabbed her purse and walked towards the door. Halfway there she stopped, and looked over at Ally. "It's not true, you know. He wouldn't do this."

"I believe you, Mee-Maw." Ally nodded. "Let's just go and see what Luke has to say."

"Yes, that would be best."

***

On the drive to the diner Charlotte was silent. Ally turned on the radio to try to soften the tension. The lyrics of the song playing were about heartbreak and lies. It didn't seem to help ease the tension in the car. She snapped the radio back off.

"Mee-Maw, I'm sure this will get sorted out."

"I hope so." Charlotte gazed out through the side window. "I just spoke with him this morning. Just this morning. How do things change so quickly?"

"When you confirmed dinner?" Ally looked over at her for a moment before turning her attention back to the road.

"Yes. We often meet for a coffee first thing in the community room at Freely Lakes before I come to work. On my days off at least we talk for ages about anything and everything. He's very easy to talk to."

"When you talked to him this morning did he tell you that he was going to the jewelry shop?"

"No, he didn't. He said he had an appointment today with a client. Then he was going to be free for the rest of the day. Free." Charlotte sighed. "I just keep picturing him in handcuffs. What an awful thought. He's such a strong, and intelligent man, to be reduced to a prisoner, it's terrible,"

"I can only imagine how difficult it is, Mee-Maw. But remember, if he's as strong as you think, he'll be able to handle it." Ally turned into the parking lot of the diner. She recognized Luke's car parked near the front. As the two walked up to the door, Luke stepped outside and held the door open for them.

"I got us a table in the back."

"Thanks." Ally noted the tight knit of his eyebrows. Her stomach twisted. Her grandmother was right, this wasn't going to be good. A waitress approached, but Charlotte waved her away.

"Luke, I'm not here to eat, I want to know when Jeff will be released."

"He will have a bail hearing in the morning." He spoke each word carefully.

"A what?" Charlotte shook her head. "This is

ridiculous, he didn't do anything!"

"You may feel that way, Charlotte, but the Broughdon police do not. They have charged him with first degree murder."

"Ridiculous!" Her voice carried through the diner and drew the attention of other people nearby.

"Mee-Maw. You have to try to calm down."

"No, I don't. Don't tell me to calm down. Jeff does not belong behind bars. You need to get him out right this instant!" She looked at Luke.

"Charlotte, I can tell you what evidence I know about. If you would like to hear it." Luke stared across the table at her.

"Mee-Maw, Luke is only trying to help."

"I know." She nodded. "Go ahead, because none of the evidence can be valid."

"The owner of a costume jewelry and jewelry supply shop, Dean Lawler, was killed this morning just after the shop opened for business."

"Dean Lawler?" Charlotte's heart dropped.

"That's Jeff's friend and Erica's father."

"Erica, the girl that comes into the shop at least once a week, right? Always orders dark chocolate covered peanuts?" Ally's eyes widened.

"Yes, that's her." Charlotte's voice trembled. "Poor girl. How did this happen? Was it a robbery?"

"I'm not sure, but I do know the murder weapon was a long metal cylinder shaped object. They believe it was a ring mandrel," Luke said.

"A ring mandrel?" Charlotte narrowed her eyes.

"Yes, it's a tool used in jewelry making to make a ring the correct size. I'm sorry to tell you this, but that ring mandrel belonged to Jeff. It was wiped clean, but he identified it as belonging to him."

"What?" She sat back in her chair. Ally slid her arm around her shoulders.

"Jeff was also seen leaving the jewelry shop in a hurry, within the thirty-minute window that the police estimate the murder took place."

"Well, that doesn't mean anything. Anyone could have come and gone in that window."

"But why didn't he tell you that he was going to the jewelry shop this morning?" Ally offered hesitantly.

"I don't know why, but it wasn't because he was planning a murder. That's insane."

"The police are interviewing him, and trying to find out more details about the incident. As far as I know he's been cooperative, but he has denied involvement."

"Of course he has." Charlotte slapped her hand lightly against the table. "Because he's innocent. Doesn't the store have security cameras?"

"Dean hadn't got around to installing them yet so there is no footage that is helpful."

"This is terrible." Charlotte shook her head. "Jeff would never do this."

"At this time he is their prime suspect." Luke

grimaced. "I do hope that changes."

"That's impossible. It's just impossible. You have to tell them that he's innocent, Luke." She stood up from the table and stared into his eyes. "You have to go there right now, and tell them that he's innocent."

"I can't do that, Charlotte, I'm sorry." Luke offered his hands, palms up.

"Why not?"

"Mee-Maw." Ally stood up. "Let's just try to figure this out."

"There's nothing to figure out. If you knew him like I do, then you wouldn't doubt it for a second. He's innocent, and he shouldn't be behind bars. Please Luke, just tell them."

"I can't," Luke said. "I would do anything in my power to help you, Charlotte, but this is something I simply can't do."

"Why?" She stepped closer to him.

"Because it will make no difference. The police have to go off the evidence, not what I tell them. The murder was in Broughdon and it's not my jurisdiction. And besides all of that I'm not sure that he is innocent." He held her gaze. "You're right, I don't know him like you do. I'm sorry if that upsets you, but the evidence..."

"Forget the evidence. He's a good man, and he is not guilty." She looked as if she might launch into more, but Ally grabbed her by the arm and steered her away from the table.

"We should go. Luke, thank you for the information." Ally tried to catch his eye, but his attention was focused on Charlotte.

"Wait, I'll walk you out." He stood up, but Ally had already guided her grandmother towards the door.

"That's all right, Luke, just let us know if you hear anything new. Okay?" Ally glanced back at him with an apologetic frown. She knew Luke had no power to influence whether Jeff was arrested or not. Her grandmother knew that, too, but she was too strong-willed to accept it.

She wanted to fix the problem as quickly as

she could.

"Yes, I will."

Charlotte nodded, but didn't speak. Instead she walked through the door and out to the car. Once settled she gazed emptily through the windshield. Ally toyed with the keys, then slid one into the ignition. As the car started she wasn't sure where to go.

"Where do you want to go?"

"Just drive, Ally."

"Yes, Mee-Maw." She pulled out of the parking lot, with no particular direction in mind.

Chapter Three

After driving a few blocks with her grandmother in silence, Ally cleared her throat.

"Do you want to go to the cottage? I'm sure Arnold would love to see you."

"No. I'll go back to Freely Lakes."

"No, Mee-Maw, we're going to go to my house, to have some tea, and talk this through. The last thing you need to see are the nosy residents trying to find out what happened."

"What's to talk about. Luke already said he's guilty."

"That's not what he said, Mee-Maw." Ally frowned. "He doesn't know Jeff and he needs to look at the evidence first, you know that."

"I do know that. But don't you agree with him?" Charlotte looked across the car at her.

"I'm not sure what happened yet, but I do know that we need to figure out what it was."

"Yes, I agree." She sighed. "I'm sorry I shouldn't have gotten so annoyed, I know Luke is only trying to help."

"Yes, he is, but I am sure that he understands why you are determined to make sure that Jeff is free. You believe he is innocent. Here we are." Ally turned the car into the driveway and parked. "You can stay here tonight if you want to keep a low profile."

"If there's one thing that these old bones have learned over the years, it's that hiding your head in the sand never solves anything. Plus, sand is really hard to get out of your ears." She cracked a smile. Ally smiled in return.

"I imagine sand crabs up your nose aren't too pleasant either."

"Ugh!" Charlotte pinched her nose and laughed as she opened the door.

Ally followed suit, then walked up the front walk. As soon as she opened the door Arnold came charging forward with a snort and a whimper.

"Aw, you know I'm out of sorts don't you, boy." Charlotte reached down to pat the top of the pot-bellied pig's head. "I've missed you, too." She sat down on the couch and the pig immediately crawled onto the couch and rested his head on her lap. "Oh, you're such a lap pig." Charlotte sighed and patted his back.

As Ally sat down beside Charlotte, her cat Peaches jumped into her lap. The two were soothed by the comfort of their animal friends as they settled into a few seconds of silence. Then Ally broke it.

"If it wasn't Jeff, then who could it be?"

"It wasn't Jeff, there's no if about it. But I don't know."

"Has he mentioned any issues with the store owner lately?"

"No, not at all. They were friends and grew up in Mainbry together. In fact Dean hosted a special showing for Jeff's jewelry just last week. Why would he do that if there were any problems between them?"

"I'm not sure, but maybe something came up between then and now."

"Nothing that could possibly turn a good man into a killer. That I don't believe."

"I'm not asking you to. Instead, let's try to figure out who else might have done it. Did Jeff ever mention that Dean had problems with anyone else?"

"No, not that I can think of." Charlotte shook her head slowly, then snapped her fingers. "Well of course there was Silvio."

"Silvio?"

"He runs a costume jewelry supply shop and since Dean opened his shop recently they were always competing for customers."

"A business rivalry?"

"Yes, but they took it a little far sometimes. Jeff mentioned once that he thought they would get into a fist fight if he didn't separate them. It made him nervous, because he doesn't like violence." She pursed her lips. "What kind of killer doesn't like violence?"

"You don't have to convince me, Mee-Maw. I think Silvio would be a great person to talk to. What about Dean's family? Was he married?"

"I don't think so. He and Jeff would go out for drinks and dinner now and then, and Jeff never mentioned a wife. He does have two daughters though. Erica of course and Jane. Erica was recently married."

"Okay, the best place to start is the suspect, let's see what we can find out about Jeff online. Maybe there is a clue there about who might want to frame him."

"I'm not sure that he'll have that much of a footprint."

"Everyone has a footprint these days." Ally did a search on his name then skimmed through the results. "Here's his jewelry website." She opened it and scrolled through some of the posts on it. "Nothing but good reviews."

"Because he's a great person and a talented

artist." Charlotte frowned. "This seems like a waste of time."

"Maybe not. Let's see what we have here." Ally clicked on another link and pulled up a social media page. "This looks like it belongs to Silvio, the owner of the other jewelry shop. Do you know Silvio?"

"I met him years ago, but I haven't seen him for ages. I don't even know if he would know who I was if we met in the street. I have never heard anybody say anything bad about him."

"There must be a mention of Jeff on here somewhere." Ally scrolled through the comments on the social media page, then raised an eyebrow. "There are three reviews here about getting better deals at Dean's shop, and two of them mention Jeff as a great designer."

"Well, that doesn't surprise me."

"Someone named Troy has replied to those reviews and claims that Jeff's designs are outdated and low quality, and that the reviewers will get what they paid for, as in cheap jewelry."

"Ugh, he has no idea what he's talking about. Who is he anyway?"

"He must be someone associated with the page to reply to the reviews. Let me check out the information page. Let's see." She scrolled through the pictures of the employees. "Aha, Troy Culpepper."

"Troy Culpepper. I know him, well I know of him and his family, not much though. He grew up in Broughdon."

"He's the assistant manager. I'm assuming in such a small shop he works directly below Silvio, and since from what it looks like here Silvio is quite a bit older, he's likely in charge of the social media accounts."

"Hey, I take offense to that." Charlotte quirked a brow. "Those of us of advanced age are just as savvy online."

"I'm sorry, I didn't mean to offend you, but Silvio looks like he's in his eighties."

"Yes, he is quite a bit older than me."

Charlotte cleared her throat. "Maybe we should go talk to them."

"We should probably wait until tomorrow. I'm sure the police are questioning everyone today. They won't be too interested in answering another round of questions so soon."

"You're right." Charlotte glanced at her watch. "It's late and most places are probably already closing. I just wish I could talk to Jeff and find out what happened."

"I'm sure you do." Ally grabbed her phone. "I'll see if Luke can help pull some strings so you can get in to talk with him first thing tomorrow. Do you know if he has anything to use for bail?"

"He just has his small business, an old car, and the apartment in Freely Lakes. I doubt that would be enough."

"Oh dear." Ally shook her head.

"Maybe I can put up the shop." Charlotte stood up and started to pace. "I can call my lawyer and find out..."

"Mee-Maw, no!" Ally looked at her with wide eyes. "You can't even think about doing that."

"Why not? I would do it in a second if it were you behind bars."

"But it's not me."

"I can trust Jeff." She sighed. "I knew you didn't believe me."

"I do believe you, Mee-Maw it's just that..."

"Just that I'm getting old?" She looked at Ally. "I'm as sharp as they come, you know that. So, do you really think I could be fooled? Lied to? Conned? I know that Jeff is a good man. I'm not some fool. I'm honestly surprised that you doubt my instincts."

"I'm sorry, Mee-Maw." She stared down at her feet. "I know that you are a good judge of character it's just that people can fool anyone. I was fooled, and lied to, and I really thought the man I planned to spend the rest of my life with was a good guy. Yes, I got conned, and sure I know that you are much smarter than me when it comes to people, but that doesn't mean it couldn't happen to you, too."

"I know, Ally. I'm sorry."

"I don't want you to believe that I doubt your instincts. It's just, I don't want to see you get hurt, the way I was or even worse."

"I understand." Charlotte met her eyes. "But that's not going to happen here. I am not any smarter than you, but I know, deep down in my heart, that Jeff didn't do this. He may tell a white lie now and then, and his ego might get the best of him at times, but murder? No, he's not capable of that. I know it's a lot to ask of you, but please, just try to trust me."

"I do trust you. More than anyone in the world, Mee-Maw. I'll make that call." She excused herself to her room to call Luke. Her heart raced as she listened to each ring. Would he be willing to help her or would he do his best to stay out of things? She wasn't sure what to expect.

"Ally, I hope you're not upset with me."

"I'm not, Luke. Honestly. Neither is Mee-Maw, she is just upset about Jeff. I need to know if we can set up a meeting for her with him."

"Yes, I'll try to arrange it for tomorrow morning, I'll let you know how I go. But I'm afraid I have some more bad news."

"What is it?" Ally held her breath.

"Apparently, they moved his arraignment up and he's been denied bail."

"Why?"

"They consider him a flight risk since he has dual-citizenship."

"Dual-citizenship?"

"Yes, here, and in England."

"Wow, I didn't know that. So, there's no chance of him getting out?"

"It's not likely until the trial."

"Trial." She sighed. "Is there any new evidence?"

"I'm looking into a few things. I'll let you

know."

"Thanks Luke. I know this was supposed to be your afternoon off."

"I'm not worried about that, but I am worried about Charlotte. Is she okay?"

"She will be. She is strong minded, she cares about Jeff and believes he is innocent."

"I'm sure that things will turn out for the best."

"I hope so." Ally hung up the phone and stepped back into the living room.

Charlotte looked up from the couch, where Arnold had settled with his head on her lap once again. "What did he say?"

"Luke is going to try and set up a meeting with Jeff in the morning, but Jeff won't be able to post bail. It was denied. Did you know that he has dual-citizenship?"

"No, I had no idea." She stared off into the distance, then looked back at Ally. "Why does that matter?"

"I guess that makes him a flight risk, so he won't be able to get out of jail before the trial."

"How terrible." Charlotte hugged Arnold. Ally's phone beeped with a text. She looked at it and turned to her grandmother.

"Luke has arranged a meeting with Jeff tomorrow morning." She sent a text back thanking Luke.

"Oh, good."

"Are you sure you don't want to stay here tonight? I'll drive you to Broughdon tomorrow."

"No thanks, I need my own bed."

"You can take my car I don't need it, I can walk to the shop in the morning."

"Thanks, I'll need you to open the shop tomorrow. I'll come in after I talk with Jeff."

"Okay. Mee-Maw, we're going to figure this out together." Ally walked her to the door. Arnold trailed after them. He nuzzled Charlotte's hand. Charlotte bent down to kiss him goodbye.

"You're a good boy, Arnold, never forget that.

You have done a good job of cheering me up." She smiled at him, then straightened up. "I hope that by tomorrow this will be settled."

"I hope so."

"I'll call you in the morning, after I speak to Jeff." She kissed Ally's cheek.

"Please be careful."

"Are you worried about me getting attacked, or arrested?" Charlotte raised an eyebrow.

"A little of both, but a little more of the arrested part."

"Don't worry, we can't both end up in jail. I have to find a way to get him out."

"And I will help you, every step of the way."

"Thank you." She smiled at her, then left the cottage.

The moment Ally sat down on the couch, Peaches climbed into her lap and Arnold snuggled next to her. Ally was comforted by their presence, once they stopped kneading and snorting. She stroked Peaches' fur.

"I just don't know what to think, guys. But one thing is for sure, we have to support Mee-Maw."

Arnold rested his head on her arm and gazed up into her eyes, then he snorted, and kicked Peaches out of her lap. The cat landed with a snarl, before the two began to chase each other around the house. Ally rolled her eyes.

"Some help you two are!"

Chapter Four

Charlotte sat up in her bed. She wasn't sure that she had ever actually fallen asleep, but she guessed she might have between bouts of wild thoughts. At some point in the middle of the night she'd considered baking a file into a cake. Instead she got dressed and headed for Ally's car.

As she walked down the long hallway to the entrance of Freely Lakes, she felt the looks of others who were already awake. She did her best to pretend she didn't notice, but it was clear that word had traveled fast. Many of the other residents at the retirement community were aware of her relationship with Jeff. Besides being seen around Freely Lakes together he was a very popular man and had insisted on taking her to dinner, and other places that they would be seen together. She didn't fight him too much either, because a part of her wanted the women that hung all over him to know that he was unavailable. But then, he wasn't really. They'd never discussed what they were to one another, they just enjoyed each other's company.

As Charlotte reached the car she tried to prepare herself for seeing him inside the police station. She hoped she wouldn't have to visit him in a cell. It made her uneasy to even think of going into a place like that. For a moment she considered calling Ally to join her, but she decided against it. She didn't want anyone there that might have the slightest doubt about Jeff's innocence. As she made the drive to the Broughdon Police Department she tried to think of the most important questions to ask him.

When she got to the station she sat in the car for a minute and tried to calm her nerves. Once she was a bit more relaxed she got out of the car and headed straight for the doors of the police station. After introducing herself she was immediately led to a small interrogation room, and instructed to wait.

As she waited she nervously tapped her fingers on the table. When Jeff was led into the room to meet her he barely looked at her as he sat down across from her. The police officer stood in the corner of the room.

"I didn't want you to see me like this."

"Imprisoned for something you didn't do? I didn't want to see you like this either." She looked into his eyes. "Jeff, are you okay?"

"Is that really what you want to know?" He gazed at her.

"Yes, of course it is."

"Not whether I did it or not?"

"Jeff, don't be silly. I know you didn't do this."

He breathed a sigh of relief. "I was hoping you would say that. I just couldn't stand the thought of you believing that I could do this."

"I would never, you should know me better than that."

"I do, but I know with Ally's boyfriend being a cop." He shrugged.

"A detective. And, I'm not here to talk about

him. I'm here to talk about you. Please, if there's anything you can tell me that will help, I'm trying to figure out what really happened to Dean. If I can do that then we will be able to get you out of here."

"I have no idea what happened to him."

"But you were there at the shop?"

"I was. I had an appointment with a client yesterday, but I realized I'd misplaced my ring sizer and mandrel. The last time I used them was at the showing that Dean hosted at his shop. I made some custom jewelry there on the spot and took orders for some items. I decided to drop by on my way to the meeting to pick up my ring sizer and mandrel. When I got there he said he didn't have them. I was going to ask to look for them, but he was busy on the phone. He got very upset, and when he hung up the phone he said he was closing and he wouldn't let me look for them. I left in a hurry because I wanted to get to the other supply store to buy new ones."

"Great! Do you have a receipt from the store?

Or confirmation from your client that you were there?"

"No, because I didn't go to either. I was about to drive to the store when my client called to cancel the appointment."

"But wait, that's still a good thing. If you spoke with your client at a certain time then that might help rule you out being at the crime scene."

"The problem is, I didn't answer. I let it go to voicemail because I was so stressed about the ring sizer. Then when I checked the message I realized I didn't even need it. I hadn't even made it three blocks away from the shop."

"So, there's no way to prove that you weren't there at the time of the murder?"

"Not one that I can think of, and to be honest, I don't think the police are interested in looking." His eyes filled with tears. He closed his eyes and pinched the bridge of his nose. "They've decided it was me, and they're not going to let this go."

"But there's so little evidence..."

"There's enough for them." He opened his eyes again. "I think it's best that you wash your hands of all of this. I don't want you to be burdened by me."

"You're not a burden, Jeff. We are friends and I care about you. I'm not going to let you waste away in here."

"Okay." He managed a small smile. "But keep in mind, not every story has a beautiful ending."

"Don't talk like that, Jeff." She looked into his eyes. "You are innocent. I'm going to find a way to get you out. What can you tell me about Silvio?"

"Silvio?" He blinked, then nodded. "Oh Silvio. He certainly was upset with Dean for all of the customers he was taking."

"Upset enough to kill him?"

"I couldn't say. I don't know Silvio that well. But I know there was a big rivalry between them."

"Anyone else? You knew Dean for a long time, didn't you?"

"Yes." He looked down at his hands with a

hint of tears in his eyes again. "His poor family."

"I'm sorry that you lost your friend, Jeff."

"So am I. I hate to think of his family thinking that I did this to him. I hate it."

"Is there anyone in his family that might hold something against him?"

"No." He shook his head. "Dean protected his family. He took care of them. They all love him. Loved." He closed his eyes again. "I'm not much help." Suddenly he opened his eyes. "Well, there was one thing."

"What's that?" Charlotte leaned forward.

"Dean and his son-in-law Brad, there was tension there. Dean told me he found out about something from Brad's past, and he was trying to decide whether to tell his daughter. He was very protective of both girls."

"Did he say what the secret was?"

"No, it was a few weeks back, our conversation was interrupted, and he never mentioned it again."

"I'll see what I can find out about it."

"Thank you, Charlotte."

"If you think of anything, just find a way to contact me. You're not alone in this, Jeff. We are going to get you out of here." She looked into his eyes.

"You really do believe me, don't you?" He held her gaze.

"Yes, I do. All of this will be over soon." She smiled at him, despite the fact that she wasn't in the least bit convinced that it would be.

***

Ally did her best to offer sunny smiles to the customers who stepped into the shop, but she wasn't feeling cheerful. She found it hard to maintain a good attitude when she was worried about her grandmother. Every time she checked her phone there were no new messages or missed calls. It made her uneasy to think of her grandmother facing everything alone and seeing Jeff in a cell. When the bell above the door chimed she looked up to see Mrs. Bing. She braced herself for the barrage of questions that would follow. Surely the rumor mill was already churning.

"Ally! I just heard the most horrifying news!"

"You did?" She gritted her teeth.

"I don't even know what to say! I am shocked!"

"It's not what you think, Mrs. Bing..."

"It isn't?" She crossed her arms. "Then you didn't give Mrs. White the first taste of a brand-new candy?"

"Oh, is that all?" Ally laughed and breathed a sigh of relief.

"I don't find it funny, not one bit. I know I've told you plenty of times to text me, call me, or flag me down when you have a new candy so I just don't understand why you didn't even bother to call!"

"They're right there in that sample tray." She pointed to the end of the counter. "I'm very sorry for the mix-up."

"That's not the point, the point is Mrs. White got to try it first." She popped a candy into her mouth. "And furthermore, mmhm." She closed her eyes. "Oh my, this is good." She pressed her hands to her chest. "What flavor!"

"I'm glad you like it. Should I put together a box for you?" Ally grinned.

"Oh, yes please." She snatched another sample from the tray.

"I'm very sorry that you didn't get the first taste. We will be trying out a new chocolate next week. White chocolate with raspberry and coconut. I'll be sure to save the first taste for you."

"I suppose I can forgive you." She sighed, and watched as Ally tossed a few extra chocolates into the box.

"Thank you." Ally smiled and handed over the box. As she rung up the chocolates, her phone buzzed. She glanced over and saw it was a text from her grandmother. "Excuse me just one moment, Mrs. Bing." She read the text and was relieved to see that she was on the way to the shop.

"Is that Luke?" Mrs. Bing fluttered her eyelashes. "Did he send you one of those kissy-mojis?"

"Kissy-mojis?" Ally laughed. "No, it was Mee-Maw saying she's on her way."

"Oh, I didn't think she was going to come in today, what with the scandal."

"Scandal?" Ally froze.

"Oh, honey everyone knows that her boyfriend got locked up. Isn't it always the case that the sweet ones fall for the bad boys?"

"He's not her boyfriend, he's just a friend, that's a man. And, we don't know that he's guilty yet."

"Right." Mrs. Bing chuckled. "Anyway, we all pick a rotten apple now and then, don't we? Do tell her that she has my support. I'd be a bit put out that Luke didn't run a background check on him though. What good is it to date a cop if he can't keep murderers away from you?"

"I'll let her know that you offered your

support." Ally forced a smile on to her lips. "Thank you, Mrs. Bing, take those on the house."

"Oh? Are you sure?" She opened the box and plucked another candy out.

"Yes. It's the least I can do, after offending you."

"True." She sniffed, then turned and walked out of the shop. Ally breathed a sigh of relief the moment she was gone. The last thing she wanted was for her grandmother to hear that kind of talk. A few minutes later a rush of customers came in. While she was waiting on them, she heard the chime of the bell again. Feeling a little overwhelmed, she looked up to see Luke. He stood off to the side, but she could tell from the heaviness of his hazel eyes that things had only gotten worse. Once all of the customers were cleared out, he walked up to the counter.

"How are you doing?" He met her eyes.

"Just tell me."

"Ally, I don't want to be the bearer of bad

news. How well do you think your grandmother really knows this man?"

"Well enough to care about him and trust him." She frowned. "They only met when she moved into Freely Lakes, he is originally from Mainbry."

"It seems to me that he has a lot of secrets. The information that comes in gets worse every time I check in with the lead detective, and Ally, you need to realize that I only have this information due to a favor from him."

"I do." She held her breath.

"I kept asking him how they could make the arrest with no motive for Jeff to kill Dean. He finally told me that they do have motive. There were some problems between them about bills being in dispute."

"That's to be expected when doing business together. I'm sure it wasn't any kind of huge issue."

"If that were the only evidence against him I

would agree, but there's more. Dean's sister, Bianca had a restraining order against Jeffrey, fifteen years ago."

"Fifteen years ago? But what does that matter now?" She frowned.

"It shows a history of issues and potential violence."

"Did he hurt her?" Her eyes widened.

"I'm not sure yet, I'm still trying to get more information on the restraining order."

The bell above the door chimed, and Charlotte stepped inside. As she looked at the two of them, her expression grew more stern. "What is it?"

"Luke was just telling me that Dean's sister took out a restraining order against Jeff fifteen years ago. Did you know about this?" Ally met her grandmother's eyes.

"No, just like he doesn't know things about me from fifteen years ago. I'm sure it was some kind of misunderstanding."

"Mee-Maw, at some point you're going to have to realize that you might not know this man as well as you think."

"This man's name is Jeffrey, and I know his heart. That's all I need to know. He is innocent, and I'm going to work to get him released. He's told me that Dean's son-in-law, Brad, had some kind of secret that might have been worth killing over. If you don't want to help, that's fine, just tell me now." She crossed her arms and looked between the two.

"Of course I'll help, Mee-Maw." Ally stepped around the counter.

"And I will do what I can." Luke slid his hands into his pockets. "Just please understand that the evidence speaks for itself, and the more that stacks up against Jeff the less likely it is that he is going to be released. It's just how it works."

"I understand that, plain and clear. I'm not asking you to do anything against the rules, Luke. Just having your support is enough."

"You have it, always." He looked into her eyes.

"I mean that. I'll look into the son-in-law and let you know if I find anything."

"Thank you, Luke." Charlotte's voice softened as she returned his gaze. "I'm sorry if I've been harsh."

"It's all right. I just want you to know that it is always my goal to put guilty people behind bars, and to keep innocent people out of prison, that is still my goal right now."

"I understand." Charlotte smiled.

Luke placed a quick peck on Ally's cheek then headed out the door. Ally wished she could spend some time with him without so much tension. But her first priority was her grandmother, who had already grabbed a pen and paper.

"Let's start by making a list of suspects."

"As of now the only lead we really have is Dean's son-in-law. If he had a secret worth keeping, then we need to find out what it was."

"You're right, but how can we do that?" Ally finished stacking the chocolates in the refrigerator.

"I say we just pay Erica a visit." Charlotte frowned.

"She just lost her father, Mee-Maw, we don't want to cause her any more pain." Ally sighed.

"I don't want to see her just to find out about her husband, but to make sure that she's safe. If Dean had reason to suspect his son-in-law was up to something and we think he might be the murderer, then Erica might be in danger."

"I hadn't even considered that." Ally's eyes widened. "If Brad did kill him, then Erica could be next. We definitely need to check in on her."

Chapter Five

Ally managed to find Erica's address easily. She lived in Broughdon. She stared at the address for some time. What if they went there and Erica knew that Jeff was friends with Charlotte? What if she was beside herself with grief?

"Mee-Maw, I found the address. But you need to be prepared for what we might find when we get there. Brad might be home and neither of them might be very welcoming."

"I know." Charlotte frowned. "I have no intention of upsetting Erica. I just want to pay my respects and to be sure she is all right. If I can get some information from her it's a bonus. I've put together a nice assortment of chocolates for her including some dark chocolate covered peanuts."

"All right, if you're ready I'm ready." Ally jotted down the address and stepped away from the computer. Charlotte picked up the box of chocolates and they headed out of the shop. Ally locked the door behind her, then hooked her arm through her grandmother's.

"We'll just stop in, Ally, nothing too intrusive. But if it leads to something, then maybe Jeff will be out by the end of the day."

"Yes, Mee-Maw, maybe he will be." Ally smiled at her, but she had her doubts. From what she had heard it was a lot harder to get out of jail than it was to get into it. They drove about thirty minutes to Erica's home. A car was parked in the driveway. Ally cleared her throat.

"So, let's just be polite and hopefully she'll invite us in."

"Can do." Charlotte stepped out of the car with the box of chocolates gripped tight in her hands. Ally prepared herself for what they might face when Erica opened the door. Losing a parent was never easy. She knocked on the door firmly, then stood back and waited to see if anyone would answer. Right away the door swung open. Erica stood in the doorway. Her eyes were swollen from old tears, and her long dark hair was pulled back in a messy ponytail. Although she looked right at Ally, Ally couldn't find the right words.

Erica was in her twenties, but it seemed to her that she had aged at least ten years since the last time she saw her in the shop.

"Hello Erica." Charlotte started to say more, but Erica sniffed and nodded.

"Charlotte, Ally. It's so kind of you to come here. I could really use some comfort food." She laughed through the tears that formed in her eyes.

"I'm so sorry about your father, Erica. We want to offer our condolences." Charlotte held out the box of chocolates. "I know it's not going to ease your grief."

"It's just what I needed. It's very sweet of you. Would you like to come in for a minute?" She stepped aside to allow them room to enter.

"Yes, thank you." Charlotte carried the chocolates inside, and Ally stepped in after her.

"Honestly, I think everyone is afraid to talk about it. When I first heard, everyone called, everyone visited, but that was over so quickly and now, it's just so quiet." She bit into her bottom lip. "My husband is handling some of my father's affairs, so here I am in this house alone, and it just seems so surreal."

Charlotte and Ally followed her into the living room. Erica gestured to the couch as she sat across from them in a chair.

"It's our pleasure to keep you company, Erica. When my daughter passed away, people did the same, the loss was so intense, I think they just didn't know how to talk about it. But I needed to talk. We're here to listen."

"I'm just so shocked by all of this. It's comforting for me to talk about him."

"We have heard that he was a wonderful man." Charlotte glanced over at Ally. "To lose a father, a parent, is so overwhelming. It's more than just a loss of a loved one, it's a loss of a life-long guardian."

"Yes." Erica grabbed a tissue and pressed it beneath her eyes as she nodded. "I can't even picture life without him."

"I've heard he was very protective of you, and your sister," Ally said casually.

"Yes, he was." She laughed. "He would greet our dates with such an interrogation that I had a few decide against taking me out when I was a teenager. It upset me at the time, but now looking back, I understand why he did it. He was a great father."

"I imagine your husband must be a wonderful person, too, if he made it past that interrogation." Ally smiled.

"Yes, he is. Although, he and my father did not always get along. I guess, my dad just didn't think any man was good enough for me." She shrugged, then stared down at her hands in her lap. "I miss him so much already."

"I'm sure you do." Charlotte offered her a box of tissues from the coffee table.

Erica sniffed as she grabbed a tissue. "Thank you for listening. I'm still numb I think. My dad was so important to me. He always told me the truth. No matter what, he was honest with me. Sometimes I would feel like he was the only one that was."

"It's so important to have people in your life that you can trust. Maybe you can turn to your family?" Ally glanced around the room at the family photographs on the walls.

"Yes, I am glad to have them, but my aunt she is a little dramatic, and sometimes she tells stories. She is on vacation at the moment, but she is cutting it short to come back for the funeral. My sister is so busy with her children right now, it's hard to get time to talk with her. And she is going through her own loss, her children have lost their grandfather, it's all very difficult. Of course, there's my husband Brad, but he's more of a doer. He is a problem solver. His way of handling my father's death is to make sure that all of his affairs are in order. Which is helpful to me, but keeps him pretty busy."

"It is nice that he's taking the lead on that.

Sometimes it's hard to go through all of the routine around someone's death. It sounds as if whatever issues they had in the past, were reconciled."

"I'm not sure. My father always mentioned to me that he thought Brad wasn't very honest. Which is true, he's kept things from me before, even lied to me about a few things, but nothing too major. My father just had very high standards when it came to honesty. But things must have been getting better between them, because they were supposed to go golfing this weekend together. It was the first time my father ever invited him to do that." She grabbed another tissue. "And now they won't be able to."

"At least your father knew you would be taken care of, maybe that can give you a little comfort." Charlotte's voice softened with sympathy. As Erica wiped away tears, Ally fought her own as the conversation brought back memories of losing her mother. She knew if she listened to the woman's grief much longer she might shed a few. As her cheeks burned, she decided to excuse herself to gather her emotions in private.

"I'm sorry to ask, Erica, but is there a bathroom that I could use?"

"Oh yes, it's just down the hall there and on the right." She pointed to a hallway filled with boxes. "Excuse the mess, we had some things from my father's office moved out of the store once the police were done looking through them. I honestly don't know what are and aren't important documents so we just brought them here for now to keep them safe."

"Thank you." Ally made her way down the hallway.

The stacks of boxes called to her. Maybe there was something in them that would give them another suspect to look into, or an indication that Brad really was involved.

Ally held her breath for a moment and listened to be sure that no one had followed her, then as casually as she could she peeked into the boxes. Right on top of one of the boxes was a customer logbook. She could see Dean's neat handwriting on every line. Quickly, she glanced up towards the living room. She could hear her grandmother offering comforting words. With a little time to spare she decided to photograph each of the recent pages of the logbook. She snapped pictures until she heard the floor creak. Someone in the living room stood up. She darted into the bathroom and tucked her phone into her pocket. As she flushed the toilet and washed her hands, her heart raced. What if she had been caught taking pictures? The thought left her unsettled. When she opened the bathroom door, Erica's voice drifted from the living room.

"Brad, I didn't expect you home so soon."

Ally's heart jumped into her throat as heavy footsteps made their way into the living room. Brad, as in the only murder suspect they had? She stepped back into the living room just in time to see a tall, thick man, tower over her grandmother.

"What are you doing here?" His voice raised with each word he spoke.

"Brad stop! Don't speak to her like that, they're just here to help." Erica grabbed on to his thick arm and tugged at him. "Why are you acting like this?"

"And how is the girlfriend of the man who murdered your father going to help you?" He shot a glare in Erica's direction. "Why did you let her in here?"

"What are you talking about?" Erica looked from Charlotte, to Ally. "They're friends of mine."

"Friends?" He growled. "I know exactly who you are." He jabbed a finger towards Charlotte. "When I was with my father-in-law in the shop Jeff was there. He was bragging about what a beautiful woman he was dating. He showed him your picture. The only reason you're here is because he's exactly where he should be, locked up!"

"Mee-Maw, we should go." Ally stepped between her grandmother and Brad.

"That's right you should go! What kind of nerve do you have coming here after what Jeff did?" He refused to move back as Charlotte got to her feet.

"Jeff didn't do this, he wouldn't do this. You know that, and I'm sure you do, too, Erica." She looked past Brad, to Erica, who's face crumpled with confusion.

"You're Jeff's girlfriend? Why did you lie to me? Why didn't you tell me?" Erica glared at her. "You said I could talk to you."

"And you can, sweetheart. I meant what I said. I didn't want to cause you any pain. Jeff was a good friend of your father's and I know that he didn't do this. Don't you want the right person to be arrested for your father's murder?"

"You need to leave. The two of you should be ashamed." Brad held Erica close in his arms as he glared at them.

"My grandmother didn't..." Ally began to defend her grandmother.

"No Ally, don't." Charlotte placed a hand on her shoulder. "Erica, I'm sorry. I truly am sorry about your loss. I can assure you that Jeff had nothing to do with this, and one day soon, you will know the truth."

"Don't you say another lying manipulative word! Just get out before I call the cops!" Brad pointed to the door. Ally steered her grandmother towards it. She glanced back just before they stepped through the door and saw Brad wrap his arms around Erica. Erica rested her head against his chest. Ally felt sorry for Erica, but she was also frightened by the thick muscles that flexed in Brad's arms. What would he do if Erica began to suspect that he was the killer?

Once in the car, Charlotte looked at Ally. "I'm sorry, Ally, maybe we shouldn't have done that."

"There's nothing to be sorry for, Mee-Maw. We were only there to pay our respects and try to find out the truth. It's clear that Brad probably has enough rage in him to commit the crime that we think he might have. I just hope that he loves Erica enough not to cause her any harm." She started the car and pulled out of the driveway. "I never expected him to know that you and Jeff were dating."

"I can't believe Jeff would show my picture around like that." Charlotte frowned. "That seems rather childish to me."

"I don't think so, Mee-Maw. It sounds like he's in love to me." Ally glanced over at her.

"Yes, well." Charlotte blushed as she stared through the window. "That's not important now."

"I know neither of us was expecting things to happen the way they did, but we'd better be more careful from now on."

"Yes, you're right, we should. Are we still going to stop at Silvio's store?"

"Yes, we're already here in Broughdon."

"Good. Maybe that will give us some more insight into what happened here." She bit into her bottom lip. "It was horrible to hear Jeff called a killer."

"Do you think Erica knew about whatever secret her husband is keeping?" Ally glanced over at her.

"I doubt it. That's why I stopped you. She just lost her father, she doesn't need to know that her husband is keeping secrets, too."

"Unless that secret is that he murdered her father."

"Yes, you're right, but without proof there's no point to accusing him."

"I did find something interesting in the boxes in the hallway. It was a logbook and it includes the most recent customers at the shop. I took pictures of the last few pages so we can have an idea of who has been in contact with Dean recently."

"Oh, that's a great place to start. Maybe he had a dispute with a customer that led to this."

"It's possible." Ally frowned. "I'm also curious about Dean's competition. If there were issues between them, maybe they got to the point of violence."

"Maybe." Charlotte nodded. "Let's go now to Silvio's supplies and see what we can find out."

As they drove towards the shop, Ally noticed how quiet her grandmother was. She reached over and patted her knee.

"It's okay, Mee-Maw. We'll work this out."

"I just hope that we can prove that someone else did this."

"We're working on it. We're going to figure it out." Ally shot her a look of reassurance, then focused on the road.

Chapter Six

The outside of 'Silvio's Supplies and More' was fairly plain. Other than a small sign above the large front window that declared its name, there was no decoration. Ally held the door for her grandmother. As they stepped into the shop they were surrounded by shelves filled with assorted jewelry making supplies. At the back of the shop a long glass counter stretched from nearly one end to the other.

"Hello there." A short man with a round face and thinning gray hair smiled at them both. "Anything I can help you with?"

"We're interested in getting a ring re-sized." Charlotte paused in front of the counter and offered him her brightest smile.

"Well then, you've come to the right place. May I see the ring?" He put on a pair of thick frameless glasses and peered through the lenses.

"Yes, here it is." Charlotte tugged the ring off

her finger and placed it down on the counter. "I'd like to give it to my granddaughter, and I want to make sure that it will fit her. My fingers are much bigger than hers."

"Oh, I understand." He smiled. "Do you know your ring size, young lady?" He glanced over at Ally.

"No, I'm sorry it's been a while since I've worn one." Ally did her best to keep up with her grandmother's ruse.

"That's no problem at all. I have this lovely device that will give us your exact size." He pulled out a box with a bundle of plain metal rings and a ring mandrel. "Just find the one that fits you the best." He handed her the bundle of rings.

"Okay, thank you." She began to slide the rings on to her finger one by one.

"Aha, getting married are you?" He smiled. "I think it's wonderful when family members pass on heirlooms."

"No, I..."

"Yes, she is." Charlotte kicked Ally's foot lightly with her own. "Something old, you know." She winked.

"Oh yes." He chuckled.

"We had an appointment scheduled with 'Dean's Jewels and Supplies', but did you hear what happened to him?" She clucked her tongue. "It's such a tragedy, but of course now we're in a bind because the wedding is so close."

"Yes, it is a tragedy. But I am glad that you came here. I can assure you that the quality of the ring re-sizing will be stellar."

"I hope so. We had hoped to use Dean's designer to create some costume jewelry for the bridesmaids. We just love his work." Charlotte glanced through the jewelry on display in the glass cabinet. "I guess you don't have anything of his?"

"No, I don't, thankfully. I would not want a murderer's merchandise in my shop."

"Wait, are you saying he's the one that killed Dean?"

"He is certainly the main suspect. Would you believe the police even came here and questioned me? But of course, I was here in my shop. I had to be, as my assistant was out on a delivery. So neither of us could have been at Dean's shop when he was murdered. It was strange to be treated like a suspect, especially when they already know who killed Dean."

"Perhaps they are mistaken." Charlotte pursed her lips.

"I think I found the right size." Ally piped up and shot a look of warning at her grandmother. She could tell from the pink in her cheeks and the tone of her voice that she was offended by the way Silvio spoke about Jeff.

"Wonderful." Silvio turned his attention to her. "Now I just take the rings and write down the size." He took the ring from her and jotted down some details. As he was doing that Ally looked at the metal mandrel in the box. Wielded with enough force it could do some serious damage. But as she watched Silvio's hand tremble when he grasped the bundle of rings she wondered if he would be strong enough to produce that much force. "And now I have your size. So, let me get the paperwork ready for the ring."

"Oh actually, we are still shopping around." Charlotte picked up the ring from the counter.

"I will make you a great deal." He raised an eyebrow and smiled.

"I will keep that in mind. We may want to come back and look at more of your costume jewelry. But this is a once in a lifetime event, we can't rush into anything."

"But I thought you said you were under pressure to get the ring done?" He straightened up and looked from her, to Ally, then back again. "Did I misunderstand?"

"No, you didn't, but we still need to think about it." Ally smiled as she met his eyes. "Perhaps you could give us a quote so we can consider how it fits into our budget."

"Yes, I can do that." He picked up a pen and

began to scribble on a pad of paper. "Do you live nearby?"

"In Blue River actually." Ally watched the way he grasped the pen as he wrote. There was no hint of the shake she saw before.

"Oh, that's perfect. Troy makes deliveries there all the time. To a little jewelry shop, maybe you know it, Jen's Gems?"

"Oh yes, Jen." Charlotte nodded. "She has some beautiful pieces."

"She does, most of her collection is from here. But she doesn't do re-sizing. Here is my estimate for the ring, and please don't be afraid to contact me if you have any questions." He handed Charlotte the slip of paper.

"Thank you for your time." Ally smiled at him. "I'm sure we'll be back."

"Wonderful, and congratulations on the wedding."

Ally bit her tongue as they walked out of the shop.

"Interesting conversation, wasn't it?" Charlotte glanced back over her shoulder through the glass door.

"Getting married? Really Mee-Maw?" She sighed.

"What? It was the best excuse I could come up with." She laughed. "He seems like a nice enough man. Or at least he pretends well."

"Yes, he does. I'm not sure that he could have murdered Dean. Did you notice how his hands shook?" Ally started to walk towards the car.

"Yes, I did. But you can't let that rule him out. Some people play up a role in order to get sympathy from a customer. He may look frail and unassuming while we're in there, but once we're gone he might be someone completely different."

"I hadn't even considered that." Ally shook her head. She was about to open the door to the car when a delivery van pulled into the parking lot. She watched as the van drove towards the back of the store.

"That must be Troy." Charlotte's gaze followed the van as well.

"Did you notice how muddy the van is? I wouldn't be impressed by a delivery van that pulled up to my business or home looking like that."

"No, I wouldn't either." Charlotte opened the car door and settled inside. Ally stuck her head inside.

"Do you think we should go talk to him? Ask him about the murder?"

"No, not now. If we start grilling him then Silvio will get very suspicious. We want to be able to come back here and ask more questions if we need to. Besides, we have another way that we can check on Troy's alibi. We can confirm with Jen, at Jen's Gems, that Troy made the delivery."

"Oh yes, that's a good idea. Why don't you give her a call?"

"I'll look up her number." Charlotte placed the call once she found it. She shook her head after the answering machine picked up. "She's closed today but she'll be open tomorrow."

"Okay, that's actually a good thing, because right now, we need some lunch, and to regroup." Ally headed towards Blue River.

Charlotte was silent for some time, Ally could tell she was lost in thought.

"Are you okay, Mee-Maw?"

"Ally, I just keep thinking about Jeff in that horrible place. What will he eat for lunch? Gruel?"

"Mee-Maw, I don't think it will be that bad. I'm sure they'll have a decent meal to offer. But I understand why you're concerned." Ally turned down the new highway that led back to Blue River. "Ouch, look at the traffic." She shook her head as she studied the stream of cars in front of them.

"Yes, it's that time of day." Charlotte glanced at the clock on the dashboard. "Lunchtime rush. Do you think that Brad will file a complaint about us with the Broughdon PD?"

"I'm not sure, but if he does, we're going to

have to be prepared for it. To be honest I'm surprised that the police haven't spoken to you about Jeff."

"I guess they feel they have enough evidence." Charlotte frowned. "It's for the best as I would likely give that detective an earful about his inability to do his job correctly."

"Now Mee-Maw, you have to admit if you saw the same evidence stacked against Jeff, you might draw the same conclusion, if you didn't know him."

"That's not true, Ally." Charlotte looked over at her. "I'm sure I would look deeper than a possible murder weapon and him being nearby the crime scene. That's not conclusive evidence."

"And the restraining order?" Ally navigated through some traffic and finally turned off the highway on to the main street that ran through Blue River.

"That's old news." Charlotte's voice lost some of its strength.

"It may be old news, but it can be relevant, it can indicate a pattern of behavior."

"Ally." Charlotte frowned. "We don't know what it was even for. Please don't assume things."

"You're right, I'm sorry." Ally pulled into the driveway of the cottage. "But you can't blame me for being protective, can you?" She met her eyes as she turned off the ignition. "You are such a beautiful person, Mee-Maw, and I just don't want to see anyone hurt you."

"I do understand that." Charlotte squeezed her hand. "But, I'm also my own person, with a few more years of experience on this earth. So please, let me decide whether or not assumptions should be made."

"All right." Ally nodded and offered her a small smile. "I love you, Mee-Maw."

"I love you, too." She kissed her on the forehead, then they climbed out of the car.

Ally and Charlotte were greeted as usual at the front door by one lively pig and one hungry cat.

"Settle down!" Ally huffed as she slipped past them inside the door. They followed her right into the kitchen. "Here, Mee-Maw, why don't you look over the pictures that I took at Erica's while I tame these wild animals."

"Sure." Charlotte took the phone Ally offered her, then gave Arnold a good ear rub. "Aw, is your little belly growling."

"His little belly is always growling!" Ally laughed. While Ally got the pets some food to eat, Charlotte began to skim through the pictures that Ally took.

"You did a great job with these pictures, Ally. I was able to get all of the names and phone numbers of recent customers at the shop. I think we should start making some calls to see if anyone noticed anything strange when they were at the shop."

"I agree, go for it. I'll be right in to help." Ally fought with Arnold to get his food in his bowl without him trying to devour the entire bag. Then she gave Peaches her little dish on the counter.

Peaches purred and flicked her tail at her. "Now you be good, Peaches and don't steal Arnold's food." She stroked her hand down the cat's back, then began to prepare lunch for herself and her grandmother. She walked into the living room with two sandwiches and two glasses of tea.

"Oh, thank you that looks so good." Charlotte took her plate and glass from Ally. "I didn't realize I was so hungry until just now."

"You go ahead and eat, I'll make some phone calls."

"This one." Charlotte pointed to a name on a list she'd written down. "His name is Chris and he was the last customer of the day the day before Dean was killed. It's a long shot, but maybe he noticed something, or Dean mentioned something to him about being worried."

"All right I'll check it out." Ally looked at the details. "Chris Rogerstons. Isn't that the name of our plumber," Ally said as she walked over to the fridge to look at the plumber's fridge magnet.

"Maybe," Charlotte said. "It sounded familiar,

but I couldn't place it."

"It is." Ally walked back into the living room.

"That's good, at least he knows us." Charlotte smiled.

"Why would a plumber want jewelry supplies?" Ally dialed Chris' number. She waited as it rang. Just when she was sure no one would answer, a breathless man picked up the phone.

"Hello, Chris' Plumbing?"

"Hi, is this Chris?"

"Yes, it is, can I help you?"

"Hi Chris, my name is Ally Sweet. I don't know if you remember me, but you fixed the boiler at my cottage a few weeks ago."

"Oh, yes. The cottage with the pig."

"That's it," Ally said with a hint of relief. Maybe it would be easier to get information out of him now.

"Is there something wrong with it?"

"Oh no, nothing to do with that, I actually just

wanted to see if you could tell me some information about the murder of ..."

"Dean? Are you talking about Dean?"

"Yes, I am. I need some information and I was wondering if you would mind telling me a little bit about him."

"I don't know, what kind? Why?"

"Someone has been arrested who I think is innocent and I think you might have been one of the last people to see Dean alive. So, I was wondering if you could offer any information that might help me learn more about him."

"All right. Well, I don't know how much I can help, I was a new customer of his."

"Oh? Is this the first time that you needed jewelry supplies?"

"Actually, I purchased costume jewelry from him, I had some custom-made pieces made there as well. I used to go to Silvio's but Dean made me such a great offer, I couldn't turn him down."

"So this was your first transaction with him?"

"Yes, it was. I was very impressed with his selection and when he quoted me the price, I just had to cancel my order with Silvio."

"Did you notice anything strange about the shop or Dean when you picked up your order?"

"No, not at all. He was very personable. He helped me load the boxes into my van and I gave him some tickets to attend the play."

"Play?"

"Yes, plumber by day, amateur play director by night." Chris laughed. "That's what I needed the jewelry for."

"Sounds interesting."

"Yes, it helps me use my creative side."

"Was there anyone else at the shop when you were there?"

"Uh, yes, now that I think about it there was. A man, I think his name was Brad?"

"Were Dean and Brad talking at all?"

"When I came in they were. It looked like

Brad was taking inventory or something. Anyway, all I can say about Dean is that he was a nice guy and gave me a great deal. I am not sure how that helps."

"It does, thanks so much for your time, Chris." Ally hung up the phone and looked over at her grandmother. "Chris just placed Brad at the shop the night before Dean was killed. He said it looked like Brad was taking inventory."

"Interesting. If Dean told him that night that he knew about the secret Brad might have been angry enough to come back the next day and kill him."

"Yes, I think you're right about that." Ally opened her mouth to say more, when a wild screech silenced her. She turned her head in time to see Peaches charge across the carpet. Arnold tore into the living room after Peaches. He squealed as loud as he could and circled the cat around the couch.

"Uh oh, Peaches must have tried to steal some of Arnold's food again." Ally rolled her eyes as the noise continued. Just then her phone began to ring.

"Mee-Maw, it's Luke calling." She picked up her phone and stepped out of the living room so that she wouldn't have to compete with Arnold's squealing.

"Hi, Luke."

"Ally, what have you been up to?"

"What do you mean?"

"I got a call from the detective heading the case in Broughdon. He said he's had a few calls about you questioning people about Dean's death. Is there a reason why you didn't tell me about this?"

"We were just asking a few questions, we didn't do anything wrong." She frowned.

"I know you didn't, but the detective is getting a little sensitive about your involvement. So far I've managed to persuade him that Charlotte doesn't know anything about the crime, but if her name keeps coming up then it is going to get more difficult."

"I understand, and I appreciate your help, Luke. We didn't mean to cause any problems. But we did find out some information." She filled him in on the encounter with Brad, the customer names she'd found, Silvio's alibi, and the information that Chris supplied.

"Wow, you got a lot accomplished in one morning. No wonder I got a call from the detective. Are you sure you don't want to wear a badge?"

"No, I'm perfectly happy with making chocolates. But what I'm not happy with is Mee-Maw being upset. I'm worried about her. Especially with that restraining order to think about."

"Well, I do have a little news about that. It turns out the restraining order was for stalking, not violence. She claimed that he was following her everywhere and calling repeatedly, however I don't see much evidence to support that."

"Well, it is a relief that there wasn't violence

involved, but it still makes me uneasy that someone could be that obsessive. What happens if Mee-Maw decides she's not interested anymore?"

"That's something to consider. But I think we need to discuss this situation with Brad. I don't want you putting yourself in a dangerous position. Brad could very well be dangerous, he's already shown quite a temper."

"Yes, I know, and he was with Dean the night before he was killed."

"How did Erica seem?"

"Upset. She had nothing but kind things to say about her father."

"What about Silvio? It sounds like he was losing a lot of business to Dean. Maybe that was enough to drive him to murder. It's not the biggest market and Dean just opened his shop recently, so maybe the new competition means that Silvio wouldn't be able to stay afloat much longer with Dean undercutting his prices and stealing customers."

"I agree, and Chris, the customer I told you about, canceled his order with Silvio and went to Dean instead. However, Silvio seems pretty frail, and he has an alibi. He was at the shop the whole time because his assistant Troy was out for a delivery. They are the only two that work in the shop."

"Interesting. But that doesn't give him an alibi."

"It doesn't?" Ally frowned.

"No, just because he says that he was there doesn't mean that he stayed there. Depending on how long Troy was gone, he might have been able to leave the shop, go to Dean's shop, kill Dean, and return as if nothing ever happened. The only way it's an alibi is if someone or something can prove that he was actually there that entire time."

"I hadn't even considered that, Luke. See, this is why you are the detective."

"Aw, thanks." He smiled. "Listen I have to go, I have a case I'm working on, but I will update you if I hear anything more."

"Thanks Luke."

"Oh, and by the way, are you at least going to propose?"

"What?" She nearly dropped the phone.

"I'm just saying, if we're getting married, it would be nice if you asked me first."

"That was just a ruse..."

"I know, I'm just teasing you." He laughed as he hung up the phone. She clutched the phone in her hand as her heart slowed down. Despite how mortified she was by Luke finding out about their ruse, she let it go after only a few seconds and refocused on her grandmother.

"Ally? I sent Arnold out back, and Peaches is in your room on her bed." Charlotte stepped into the kitchen. "What did Luke have to say?"

"He made an interesting point that Silvio might not have an alibi after all. He also said that the restraining order against Jeff, was not for violence but for stalking."

"Stalking?" Charlotte scrunched up her nose.

"I can't see that happening."

"Maybe not, but what's important right now is that we keep ourselves safe. Luke thinks that Brad might be a loose cannon, so we should stay away from him."

"But we can't do nothing at all. Maybe we should go back and talk to Troy tonight."

"I don't think so, Mee-Maw. Luke said the detective on the case is already upset about how much we're interfering. He said if your name keeps coming up, the detective is going to want to talk to you."

"Well, I'm not afraid of that. I'd happily talk to the detective." Charlotte shrugged.

"Either way I think it's best if we wait until tomorrow to ask any more questions. We can go back tomorrow and speak to Troy under the guise of looking at more of the costume jewelry that's available."

"Okay, that sounds like a good plan. I think I'm going to go speak with the detective."

"What? Why?" Ally looked over at her.

"Why not? He needs to know what kind of person he has locked away without sufficient evidence. I don't want him to think that no one supports Jeff."

"Mee-Maw, I don't know if that's a great idea."

"I have nothing to hide. Maybe something I have to say can help his investigation, or at least open his mind to looking for other suspects."

"Maybe, but I'm not sure that you're going to get the welcome or the reaction that you're hoping for. He might probe you for information to use against Jeff." Ally placed her hand on Charlotte's shoulder. "As involved in this as you are, I'm just worried he could get you riled up enough to say something that you don't mean."

"The only things I could possibly say about Jeff are positive. I'm not afraid of any detective." She clenched her jaw.

"Okay." Ally squeezed her shoulder. "Then I

should go with you."

"No Ally, I need to go by myself. This is just something I have to do. Besides it would be good if you could go and organize some of the chocolates for that big order we have going out on the weekend for the new café in Mainbry."

"Yes okay, I should get a start on it." Ally nodded. "Promise you'll call me if you run into any issues?"

"Ally?" She looked into her granddaughter's eyes. "Are you afraid I'm going to end up in handcuffs?"

"I know how strong-minded you are and that you care about Jeff." Ally gazed back at her. "I'm worried that you'll put yourself at risk in order to protect him."

"I won't. I know he wouldn't want me to. You don't have to worry, sweetie. I may be angry about this, but I'm not going to take a detective hostage or stage a jailbreak, I promise." Charlotte laughed.

"Good." Ally hugged her.

"I have a bit of time, so I might take Arnold for a quick walk first. I need a bit of exercise and from the sound of that snorting so does he." She gestured to the back door.

"Good idea, Mee-Maw."

Chapter Seven

Charlotte stepped out the door with Arnold on his leash. Seeing how happy he was certainly helped calm her.

"Charlotte! Charlotte!" Charlotte turned to see Mrs. White waving her hand in the air and walking fast down the sidewalk towards her.

"Mrs. White."

"Hi Arnold." Mrs. White patted the pig's head. "Do you mind if I walk with you?"

"That would be nice."

"I need to calm down a bit."

"Why, is something wrong?" Charlotte looked at her.

"Oh, I shouldn't gossip, but it's just that I just heard something and I have to share it. Mrs. Bing and Mrs. Cale are busy."

"You can tell me if you want." Charlotte was hoping for something to distract her.

"I shouldn't, but I know I can trust you. But you can never share it please, except you can tell Ally, I know you can't keep anything from her."

"Of course, my lips are sealed." Charlotte tugged at Arnold's leash as he sniffed a tree.

"I was just talking to Mrs. Pepperston, Brad's mother."

"Erica's mother-in-law." Charlotte's eyes widened.

"Yes, she is a good friend of mine, we grew up in Broughdon together. You will not believe what Brad just told her."

"What?"

"Well, a long time ago Brad was dating Betty Grober and Betty has a five year old son," she said quickly.

"And?" Charlotte looked at her quizzically.

"And, Betty's son is Brad's," she blurted out the words then covered her hand over her mouth as if she could not believe what she had just said.

"Really?"

"Yes, poor Mrs. Pepperston is in such shock, she had no idea. Apparently, Brad has been keeping it secret from everyone."

"Until now? Why did he tell her now?" Charlotte asked casually, could this be the secret that Dean knew about. "Why didn't he tell her before?"

"Apparently, he's been planning to tell her for ages, when the time was right, but the time was never right. He has told Erica as well."

"Did he tell her before or after Dean was murdered?"

"I asked the same thing." Mrs. White nodded. "After apparently, he said that he has always planned to tell Erica and Dean."

"That's what he says now. Do you know much about Brad?"

"Not much, he is quite an offish fellow, not very friendly so I try to keep clear of him."

"So, do you think that maybe Brad killed Dean because of the secret?" Charlotte asked quietly.

"I don't think so, if he is prepared to reveal the secret now," Mrs. White said as they stopped while Arnold sniffed another tree.

"But maybe in the heat of the moment, in an intense argument, Brad simply lost his temper." Charlotte frowned. "If Dean knew about the child, maybe he tried intimidating the old man into keeping the secret or into thinking that he had to hand over his business."

"Old man?" Mrs. White shook her head. "I don't think we're talking about the same Dean here. That old man has quite a reputation and a history with the police. He has always been a force to be reckoned with and I can't imagine anyone intimidating him."

"You knew him well?"

"I used to. We went to school together, grew up together. But I haven't been very friendly with him for years now. Ever since he started getting into trouble."

"Interesting?"

"I better get going I've got rehearsals for the play."

"Is that the same play that Chris Rogerstons is working on."

"Yes, it is." Mrs. White nodded. "Thanks for listening. Feel free to stop by the theatre and have a look if we are rehearsing."

"Thanks." Charlotte tugged Arnold's leash so they could turn around. She quickly walked back to the cottage, mulling over what she had learned from Mrs. White.

When she reached the cottage she wanted to tell Ally what Mrs. White had told her, but she had already left for the shop.

Charlotte said good-bye to Arnold and Peaches and decided to head to the police station in Broughdon to see the detective before she lost her courage.

As confident as she'd been with Ally about seeing the detective, she hadn't entirely convinced herself. The truth was she was upset with the detective on the case. She'd never met him, but she already knew she didn't like him. Why? Because he'd locked up the wrong man. To her that meant he wasn't very good at his job. Though, if she was honest with herself, she knew that the evidence the detective had against Jeff was convincing. When she reached the Broughdon Police Department she parked, and stared at the large building where she had just recently visited Jeff. Once she went in and spoke to the detective, all of the things Ally warned her about were going to happen probably would. After a deep breath, and a mental pep talk she stepped out of the car. When she opened the door to the police station she found that it wasn't very busy. The desk sergeant was focused on the magazine in his hand and didn't bother to look up when she approached.

"Hello? I'd like to speak with a detective, please."

"What kind of report are you making?" He began to sift through paperwork, still without looking up at her.

"I'd like to speak to him about a case he's working on."

"Do you have new information on the particular case?" He finally looked up, though his disinterest was clear in his expression. "Can you tell me a little bit about why you want to speak to a detective?"

"It's regarding the murder at the jewelry supply store." She shifted uncomfortably from one foot to the other.

"I'm Detective Russell, why are you asking for me?" A man stepped out of the side hallway. He leaned his elbow on the desk and settled his gaze on her.

"My name is Charlotte Sweet, and I would like to speak to you about your current case."

"Ah, Jeffrey's girlfriend." He smiled and gestured to a nearby cubicle. "I was planning on speaking to you sometime today. Let's chat."

"Thank you." Charlotte sat down in a chair in

front of the desk, and he sat down behind it.

"So, how long have you known Jeffrey?"

"Not too long, but I do know him very well."

"How long is not too long?"

"Several months."

"So, you don't want to give me a straight answer?" He smiled. "I guess I should think of another way to ask you."

"How long I've known him doesn't matter. The point is I do know him, and I know that he didn't commit this crime."

"Were you with him during the time of the murder?" He held her gaze.

"No, I wasn't."

"Then you can't tell me that he didn't do it. He was found near the scene of the crime, witnessed leaving in a hurry, a ring mandrel was used as the murder weapon and his was next to the body, and he had a history of conflict with the victim. Can you disprove any of that?"

Charlotte pursed her lips. She considered each of the items carefully, and had to admit that she couldn't.

"No, I can't. But I do know that he is innocent."

"Until you can tell me something a little more substantial than that, there's nothing I can do for you."

Charlotte wanted to tell him about Brad's son, but she didn't want to break Mrs. White's confidence. Why would he kill Dean over a secret he was apparently willing to reveal?

"No, there's nothing." Charlotte looked at her hands on the table.

"All right, if you say so." He shrugged.

"Is there any chance that I can see Jeff while I am here?"

"You could, but he's not here. He was transferred to Broughdon Prison this morning."

"Oh no," Charlotte said quietly. She wanted to say a lot more, she wanted to protest but she knew it would do no good.

"Let me know if you think of anything. In the meantime, I need to get back to work." He offered his hand. "Thanks for coming in."

She shook it, as she stood up from her chair. She turned on her heel, and left the police station. Things did not go exactly the way she hoped. In fact, she found herself unsettled by the detective's revelations. For just an instant, as she settled in the car, she wondered if she might be wrong. Could Jeff be the killer that the detective suspected he was? There was one piece of evidence against Jeff that really threw her. The restraining order from Dean's sister. Was there something in their past that could have come back to haunt Jeff? She decided she couldn't wait any longer to find out. With so much conflicting information stacking up, she needed to know the truth, once and for all.

**

Ally looked up the moment Charlotte stepped into the house. She closed her computer and stood up to greet her. Charlotte was pleased to see that Ally was already back from the shop.

"How did it go?"

"Well, I'm not in handcuffs, am I?" She smiled, then hugged Ally. "Honestly, I don't think the detective is looking at anyone else for this."

"Oh Mee-Maw, that's terrible."

"It is and Jeff was transferred to the prison this morning."

"Things just seem to be getting worse and worse."

"I did find out something interesting though when I ran into Mrs. White while I was out on Arnold's walk."

"You did?"

"I think that Brad's secret is that he has a son from a previous relationship."

"Okay." Ally's eyes widened.

"Mrs. White said that Brad told Erica and his mother about the son recently, after Dean was murdered. She also said that Dean had quite the reputation, and is the one that usually does the intimidating."

"Interesting?" Ally frowned. "But that doesn't mean that Brad couldn't have killed him."

"No, it doesn't, but the fact that Brad told his mother and Erica all about his secret, a son that his wife didn't know about, leaves him with not much motive. Even if he didn't really plan to tell them, a secret like that doesn't stay secret forever, no matter what you do to cover it up. So why would he kill Dean over it."

"Sometimes people don't think that far ahead though. I still think there is motive there."

"I agree, we can't eliminate him entirely. I also never knew that Dean was such an intimidating figure, Jeff never told me about that. I feel guilty about it, but I am honestly starting to doubt that he was actually as truthful with me as I had assumed. I want to know the truth about what happened between him and Dean's sister. I need to go speak to Bianca myself."

"No way, Mee-Maw, that's a very bad idea." Ally frowned. "Can't you see how that might go wrong?"

"You don't know that, Ally." She met her eyes. "As you told me, I need to be aware of Jeff's past, and this is the best way for me to be aware of it."

"But I doubt that she is going to have anything good to say about Jeff. Do you really want to put yourself through that?"

"For the truth. Yes." Charlotte shook her head. "I just can't imagine Jeff ever doing anything like that, and I want to see her face when she tells me that he did. I want to know if she's lying. Is that so wrong?"

"No, I don't think it's wrong, but I do think it's risky. Once you speak to her, you're not going to be able to turn back time and forget what she says. Are you willing to face the truth if it's not what you expect?"

"Yes." She sighed. "I don't want to even think about it, but either way, I need to know. I've never been one to shy away from the truth, you know that."

"All right, but if you're going to speak to her, then I'm going with you."

"Ally, you don't have to do that, it might be better if I talk to her by myself."

"I promise you, it will not be. It's better to have a buffer. Plus, I can be more impartial than you. Don't you trust me?" She smiled.

"You know I do, Ally. All right, we'll go together." Charlotte sat down on the couch with a sigh. "I think that visit took more out of me than I realized."

"We'll go tomorrow, after we go back and talk to Troy. I want to make sure we have ruled Silvio out as a suspect."

"After talking to that detective today, I don't think he has any interest in finding another suspect. He likes Jeff for the crime and he's going to push for him to be convicted. It just makes me feel terrible that he is all alone."

"I know that must be daunting. But I do

believe that innocent people can be protected by the system as long as they follow it. That's why we have to be careful about how we investigate. We don't want to risk tainting any evidence."

"Yes, I agree with you. Speaking of evidence, after seeing Silvio with a ring mandrel it struck me that many people could be in possession of one. Just because they found Jeff's ring mandrel there, that doesn't necessarily mean it was the murder weapon."

"Wow, I hadn't considered that, but you're right. As far as I know the only reason they considered it the murder weapon is because it matches the wound. It was wiped clean, maybe they didn't find any evidence on it. I'll double-check with Luke to make sure that's true. If that's the case, they might not have the murder weapon after all."

"I'm not sure how much that would help though. It might not make any difference unless we find the actual murder weapon, presuming it's not the one they already found at the scene."

"You're right." Ally frowned as she sent a text to Luke. "But right now, no one is looking for it. At least we will be."

"That's a good point. We know Silvio has one. I'm guessing other people in the same line of work have them, too. Silvio's store also has jewelry making supplies so maybe he has them in stock as well. Jeff was sure he left his at Dean's shop, so it's not surprising it was found there. But Dean was so distracted by a phone call that he wouldn't even look for it."

"Interesting. I wonder who he was talking on the phone with. I'll ask Luke if there is any way he can look at the phone records for that day from the shop."

"Good idea." Charlotte nodded. "Why don't I put some dinner together for us?"

"I think that would be great. Luke is texting me back. Let's see." She skimmed over the response. "He says there was no evidence found on the ring mandrel, but it was found nearby the body, and its size matches the size of the wound.

It was wiped clean. Also, he can't get the phone records, but he's sure the detective would have looked at them. He'll have a word to the detective about checking to see who was last in contact with Dean."

"That's a start." Charlotte stepped into the kitchen. "It may not be the smoking gun, but it's a start."

"Yes, it is." Ally sent a text back to thank Luke and ask him if he knew Bianca's address. He replied almost immediately. "Mee-Maw, Luke just replied. It looks like Bianca is on vacation."

"Oh no, another dead end. I think that Erica mentioned that her aunt was on vacation."

"That's right. Hopefully she'll be back soon, she is meant to be back for the funeral. Let me see if I can find out more about Dean's phone records." Ally began to search the internet to see if there was any way to get the phone records from Dean's shop. After some digging she found that many companies offered internet accessible records to their customers. If she knew his account number and password, she could possibly log into that record.

Unfortunately, she didn't even know which phone company he used, and had no idea what his account number or password might be. She gave up and joined her grandmother in the kitchen for dinner.

Chapter Eight

The next morning Ally and Charlotte headed out just after breakfast. It was still early enough that there were a few delivery trucks on the road. As they neared Silvio's shop Ally recalled the ring mandrel he had. Was it possible that was the murder weapon? If so, he had certainly cleaned it up.

Ally parked beside the delivery van. She noticed that the tires were still quite muddy. It had rained two days before, but it seemed strange for the mud to look rather fresh. Charlotte was already out of the car by the time Ally pulled the keys out of the ignition. She followed after her grandmother, and joined her inside the store.

"Can I help you?" A young man, with thin wire-rim glasses, stepped out from the back room.

"Troy?" Ally smiled as he approached the counter. Charlotte began to look through the jewelry on display.

"Yes, I'm Troy." He smiled at her in return.

"We were here yesterday to discuss the possibility of having a ring re-sized. We spoke to Silvio."

"Oh yes, he mentioned you. Did you come to a decision?" He glanced over at Charlotte, who continued to look through the jewelry.

"We'd like to see a bit more of your costume jewelry. We'd rather do everything with the same supplier and we want to make sure that you have the jewelry that would work with the wedding."

"I understand, I'll bring out some more trays from the back."

"Isn't Silvio here?"

"Oh no, he had a breakfast meeting with a client this morning. He won't be back until eleven. Would you like to make an appointment to meet with him?"

"No, that's all right. But Silvio mentioned you go out on deliveries, often to Blue River, where we're from. How do you do that if Silvio is not in the store? Do you close up?"

"Oh no, Silvio is always here if I go out on deliveries. One of us always has the store open. It's against our policy to close up early or during the day." He laughed. "Silvio and I are dedicated to our customers and making sure the store is always opened as promised."

"It's good to know that you're available so often. Isn't it dangerous for you to work alone though?" She cringed. "I've seen so many movies and television shows where stores like this are robbed."

"We're very careful, I can assure you."

"Because if we do decide to have the ring re-sized here, I don't want to find out it was stolen." Charlotte met his eyes for the first time. "Do you have security cameras and an alarm?"

"We do have both, we have an alarm and security cameras out back. Silvio has always taken security very seriously. I can assure you that security is our number one priority, and anything you leave here, will be locked away in our vault."

"Vault?" Ally tilted her head to the side. "Now that does sound secure."

"Yes, it was pretty expensive, but worth every penny. Like I said Silvio takes security very seriously. Your ring would be safe and sound here. Shall I draw up the papers?"

"I think we need a little more time to think about it." Charlotte pursed her lips. "But we'll probably be back."

"Is there anything I can do to sweeten the deal?" Troy held her gaze. "Maybe a special gift for the mother-of-the-bride?"

"Grandmother." Charlotte smiled.

"Not possible." He shook his head. "You're far too young to be a grandmother."

"Aw, you're so sweet." Charlotte batted her eyes.

"Don't I know you from somewhere?" He looked at Charlotte.

"Maybe the chocolate shop in Blue River, I own it."

"Oh, that's right."

"Do you think you could check my ring size again? I'd like to make sure that I'm getting the right size." Ally glanced at her grandmother, then back at Troy.

"Oh sure, no problem." He pulled out a ring sizer and mandrel, the same one that Silvio had used the day before. "I know everything needs to be perfect on your special day."

"Perfect." Ally nodded with a small smile. He handed her the rings and she slid the rings on one by one until she found the right size. "This one." She showed him which ring.

"Okay, let's take a look." He looked at the ring Ally had chosen. "Let's see." He glanced between it, and a piece of paper on a shelf below the counter. "Yes, it's the same, Silvio got it right, of course."

"That's good that it's been confirmed," Ally said.

"Now we know for sure that we have the

correct size. I do hope that you'll consider having your ring re-sized here."

"We will consider it." Charlotte nodded, then looped her arm around Ally's. As they walked to the car, Charlotte spoke in a quiet voice. "What were you up to in there?"

"I wanted to see the mandrel again and to see if maybe Troy had his own ring-sizer and mandrel. I'd assume that if Troy had his own, he would have used it. So, that means they likely only have one."

"True." She climbed into the car.

As Ally buckled her seat belt she looked over at her grandmother. "Unfortunately, we still have no way to confirm that Silvio was here during the murder. I say we try out the drive from here to Jen's Gems and see how long it takes. Then we can drive back, and we'll have a pretty good idea of how long it took for Troy to make the delivery and return. That will at least give us the window as to when Silvio was alone."

"It's a start." Charlotte nodded.

Charlotte and Ally climbed into the car.

"Okay, so we're Troy, and we're leaving the parking lot. Can you use a stopwatch on your phone?"

"Yes, I have one. Let me set it." Charlotte skimmed through her phone until she had the stopwatch on the screen. "You tell me when."

"Troy leaves the shop, he loads things into the van, he gets into the van, and he starts the engine, now." Ally turned on the car. Then she backed out of the parking spot. She followed the same route that she normally would. As they drove, Charlotte kept her eyes on the stopwatch.

"He wouldn't need that much time, would he?"

"I wouldn't say that. The shops may only be twenty minutes apart, but it would have taken time to get into the shop, confront Dean, and have that confrontation evolve into a murder. I'd say he'd need at least twenty minutes to commit the murder. Then keep in mind that he had to get back to the shop, and make it look like he'd never left. I'd say he'd need about an hour at least."

"Well, we're here at Jen's Gems, that took us twenty-six minutes. If Troy turned around and drove back, that would be another twenty-six minutes. A tight window."

"Right, but Troy didn't just pull into the parking lot. He hand-delivered the items, and I'm sure spoke with Jen as he did."

"Okay let's go in, and confirm she received the delivery, that should be about the same amount of time." Charlotte stepped out of the car with the stopwatch still running. They made it to the door in under thirty seconds, and were inside before the next minute passed.

"Welcome." Jen smiled as they stepped through the door.

"Jen, hi." Charlotte walked up to the counter.

"Oh, Charlotte, how are you. Still making those delicious chocolates?" She laughed. "It's been too long."

"Yes, I know it has. I've been a little busy, and

I can see you have, too. What a nice selection of gemstones you have here." She glanced around at the range of gems in small clear boxes that lined the walls.

"Yes, I love it."

"Listen, we're kind of in a rush, but we heard that you use Silvio's Supplies. I wondered if you had a good experience with him."

"Oh yes, he's great. A little more expensive than some of the competition, but it's worth it for the friendly service and the quick delivery."

"Oh? Have you had anything delivered recently?"

"Yes, just two days ago. Troy brought me some supplies. He's so great. Adorable." She laughed.

"He is quite handsome." Charlotte smiled. "So how was he when he dropped things off? Did you two have a chance to chat?"

"No, not that time. He was in a rush. He told me he had to hurry back to the shop for a meeting with a client."

"Oh, I see."

"We have to go, Mee-Maw, or we're going to be late."

"Thanks for the information, Jen. I'll be sure to come back and visit with you soon, I'll bring chocolates, too."

"Great! Thanks so much. I highly recommend Troy and Silvio!"

"Thank you." Ally opened the door for her grandmother then hurried to the car. As they climbed in she threw the car in reverse. "How are we on time?"

"Just over thirty-five minutes now, if we hurry back we should be there within the hour."

"Okay, I'm gunning it." Ally stepped on the gas. "But one thing I don't understand is that there was no mention of there being a meeting around the time of the murder."

"No, but I'm not sure that anyone checked. So, if Silvio had a meeting that Troy needed to get back for, then he was in even tighter time constraints. He was desperate for clients so I doubt he would risk not being there on time to meet one."

"You're right." Ally shook her head. "Silvio is looking less and less suspicious."

"And we just confirmed Troy's alibi. There wouldn't be enough time for him to get back from Jen's Gems to commit the murder and be there in time for the meeting with the client." Charlotte frowned. "I guess we only have one suspect left."

Ally glanced over at her and bit into her bottom lip. The truth was they had two. The last thing she wanted to do was upset her grandmother by pointing that out, but it was important to consider. As suspects were crossed off the list, Jeff remained near the top.

Chapter Nine

Later that day Ally prepared dinner to share with Luke. Arnold and Peaches hung out in the kitchen with her as she hummed her way through boiling some pasta. The more she hummed, the clearer her thoughts became. Despite the evidence piled up against Jeff, her grandmother still had faith that he was innocent. That held a lot of weight in her mind. The only question was, would she be able to find a way to prove that her grandmother was right? A light knock on the front door silenced her humming.

"Luke, come on in, I'm in the kitchen."

"Hi there." He smiled as he walked into the kitchen and set down a bag of rolls on the counter. "Fresh from the bakery, I thought they might be nice with dinner."

"Great thinking." She kissed his cheek. "Dinner is just about ready."

"How are you?" He rubbed his hands across

her shoulders as she turned back to the pot on the stove.

"I'm doing okay. I hope you're hungry, as I might have overestimated the amount of pasta we needed."

"I'm starving." He dropped down into one of the chairs at the table. "I've been running around on a case and haven't stopped for much to eat."

"Really? What case?"

"This one." He cleared his throat.

"You mean Jeff's case?" She looked over her shoulder at him.

"Yes. I just can't seem to leave it alone. I keep turning over rocks, hoping to find something that will put all of this to rest one way or the other."

"And?" She switched off the burner, and carried the pot over to the sink to drain it. As the steam rose around her face she felt a hint of comfort. She hadn't realized how tight her muscles were.

"And, I haven't been able to turn up much.

However, I did find out that there was a threat against Dean made a few months ago. Shortly after he opened the shop."

"A threat? By who?"

"We're not sure who. The incident was reported to Broughdon PD, but nothing was ever done about it."

"I don't understand, why not?" She prepared them both a plate and carried them to the table. "If he was threatened shouldn't something have been done?"

"Unfortunately, the threat was anonymous. Someone spray-painted all over the back of the shop. They used words like, criminal, thief, even went so far as to threaten to burn down the building. The police investigated, but they never came up with anything."

"I don't understand why Dean didn't have cameras throughout the store. Surely that would be a priority."

"Well, when people don't have cameras it's

usually because they're involved in something that they don't want recorded." He quirked a brow. "It's possible that Dean was still involved in some underhand dealings. If that is the case there may be an entire pool of suspects that we're not aware of."

"So, the Broughdon PD never had any idea who could have done it?"

"I think there was just an assumption that it was some kind of prank pulled by some local kids. There is a bit of a graffiti problem in the area. Honestly, I just don't think it would have taken priority, as long as there was another more important case to work on, they probably didn't concentrate on the graffiti."

"That's a shame. Maybe if they had pursued it, they would have figured it out before Dean was killed."

"It's a possibility, but I can't say that I wouldn't have done the same thing. Graffiti seems like just graffiti. There wasn't any violence involved, and Dean claimed he didn't have any issues with anyone. Of course, that could have easily been a lie, but if he knew who did it, he wasn't forthcoming with Broughdon PD about it."

"Maybe he was used to handling his own problems." She frowned and pushed a fork through her food.

"Maybe, or maybe he didn't take it seriously either. These things do happen on occasion."

"I guess." She pushed at her food again, without taking a bite.

Luke studied her from across the table. "Are you okay?"

"Yes, just a little distracted."

"I can see that you're really troubled about something, just talk to me." He pushed his plate aside and reached his hand across the table. She placed her hand in his and looked up at him.

"I'm worried about Mee-Maw. She's so determined that Jeff is innocent of this crime, and honestly I believe he might be, but that doesn't make him a good man. Does it?"

"I guess that depends on what you think makes a good man."

"He's kept many things from her." She shook her head. "That doesn't seem like a good man to me."

"Their friendship is new. It takes time for people to confide in each other. There are things that we don't know about each other. I don't think he's actually lied to her that you know of, has he?"

"No, it's just this feeling I have. Like maybe, he's hiding something from her. I mean, what if we're all wrong, what if he actually did this?" She locked her eyes to his. "What if I'm helping to free a murderer?"

"I can see why you're concerned." He traced his fingertips along the length of her hand. "Is there anything I can do to help?"

"I want to speak to him myself."

"Are you sure about that?" He lifted an eyebrow. "It might not be the best way to get to know him, behind bars."

"I need to see what Mee-Maw sees in him. I need to look into his eyes and hear him tell me that he's innocent, so I can put all of this worry to rest. Do you think they will let me see him?"

"More than likely. I can pull some strings and have it set up for you. I'll come with you."

"He might not be willing to talk too much to me if you're there. I think it's better if just I go."

"Okay, if that's what you want, that's fine."

"Honestly, I'm not sure if it's what I want, but I don't see any other options. I need to get to the bottom of this."

"All right, I'll set it up for you." He pulled his plate back in front of him. "Now why don't you tell me about what else is going on in your life? Maybe a little distraction will help us both to remember there is a world beyond this case."

"Hm." She closed her eyes for a moment. "Well, Mrs. Bing was very upset with me for letting Mrs. White sample a new chocolate before her."

"Oh no. Did she get violent?" He laughed.

"No, not quite." Ally grinned. "Oh, and I have to take Arnold to the vet. He's due for his check-up. He's not going to be too happy about that."

"Aw, poor Arnold. He has such a hard life, with all of the snuggling and treats."

"Yes, maybe a few too many treats and not enough exercise. Last time Mee-Maw was there the vet warned her to watch his weight, and I can't say I've done that."

"He's a pig." He shook his head. "Now even pigs are getting body-shamed?"

"Very funny." She grinned. "But we want him to stay as healthy as possible. Hopefully, she'll have some good advice for me."

"When is his appointment?"

"The day after tomorrow. Hopefully by then, we'll know a little bit more about what is going on with the murder."

"Ouch, you did it." He sighed.

"What?" Her eyes widened.

"You managed to make Arnold's appointment about the case. We were supposed to be distracting ourselves, remember?"

"Oh right." She groaned. "I guess it's impossible."

"Well, there are other ways." He set down his fork and met her eyes across the table. "Want to take a walk with me after dinner?"

"Yes, that sounds lovely."

"Good."

As they finished their food there was a transition in the conversation, from strained, to more relaxed. Ally couldn't resist the way he smiled at her, or the touch of his hand against hers. She could tell that he was trying to draw her out of her funk and remind her that things would get better. After the dishes were cleared away, they put Arnold on a leash and stepped outside into the last of the evening light.

"Isn't Charlotte staying with you?"

"No, she wanted to stay in her apartment. I

think she needed some space to collect her thoughts."

"She must have a lot on her mind with all of this."

"You know, when she first mentioned Jeff I thought she had to be joking. I never imagined her being in a relationship with someone. But these past few weeks I've seen such a change in her. I can see how happy he makes her. She's still independent and her own person, but he adds an extra dimension to her life." She sighed as she looked up at the sky. "I just hope that doesn't change."

"I don't think it will. I'm sure this will get cleared up soon." He wrapped his arm around her shoulders. "There's still time to prove that Jeff is innocent, if he is."

"Yes." She smiled and met his eyes as Arnold snorted. "That's what I need to keep in mind. You always stay so calm."

"I try to stay calm. But I can't always. A calm mind allows me to think things through and get to the truth easier. But in certain situations, it's impossible."

"I imagine it is. You must face so much while you're at work."

"Things tend to be pretty quiet, but there are moments."

"Luke, will you be honest with me about something?"

"Sure." He paused and turned to look at her.

"When you first heard about Jeff, and Dean's murder, what did your instincts tell you?"

"Ally, that's not really a fair question." He shoved his hands into his pockets. "I'm not sure I can answer it."

"You have so much experience working with criminals. I know you are a great investigator. All I want to know is what your first gut instinct was about Jeff. I promise not to hold your answer against you."

"Honestly?" He ran his hand back through his hair, then looked off down the street.

"Yes, honestly." She took his hand and gave it a light squeeze.

He looked back at her. "My first thought was, no way, Charlotte would never be interested in someone capable of murder. I trust her instincts, but anyone can be fooled and as I reviewed the evidence against him, that changed, and I began to believe that he conned her. If Jeff's girlfriend had been anyone else, I wouldn't have even thought twice about him convincing her he was a good person. But since it was Charlotte, my judgment was clouded."

"And now?" She searched his eyes. "What do you think now?"

"I think that even the best instincts need to be tempered by the evidence. I think until we can prove otherwise, the evidence points to Jeff."

"But you still really think he could be proven innocent?"

"Yes, I do." He smiled and brushed a few strands of her hair back from her face. "You wouldn't be fighting so hard for someone who was guilty, Ally. You may not know it yourself, but your instincts are telling you he's innocent."

"I think they are." She bit into her bottom lip. "I just hope that I'm not wrong."

As they continued their walk along the street, she thought about all of the people living their lives in their homes. If Jeff was innocent, and locked away, what did it mean to them? Did it mean that any one of those people could be caught up in a similar miscarriage of justice at any time? It made her uneasy to think that was possible. If Jeff was innocent, she had to make sure that he was set free.

Chapter Ten

Early the next morning Ally woke up to snorting right beside her ear. For just a second she thought she might be imagining it, until she recognized the pig breath.

"Oh Arnold, it's too early." She gave the pig a light shove which only inspired him to lick her cheek. "Ugh, gross." She sighed then opened her eyes. He gazed into her eyes with such affection that she couldn't stay mad at him. "You silly pig. You are always getting into something, aren't you? You heard me talking about your appointment with your vet last night, I bet. That's why you're so anxious." She sat up and patted his head. "Nothing to worry about, Arnold, it's just a check-up. I'm sure she will say you are just as healthy as always. Especially if we make sure that you have your breakfast."

As soon as the word breakfast escaped her lips, Peaches gave a plaintive meow from the bottom of the bed where she was curled up.

"Yes, yes, I know you're hungry, too. Just because it is two minutes after seven, that doesn't mean that you're starving." She climbed out of bed and grabbed a robe to stave off the chill of the morning air. Both animals followed her right into the kitchen with their own versions of begging to remind her that they were about to pass out from hunger. She rolled her eyes and set about feeding them both. Only after they were quiet, did she recall that she had a meeting with Jeff that morning.

Luke texted her the night before with the appointment time, and his final offer to go with her to the meeting. She'd declined, but was glad he'd offered. Luke had such a sweet way of never letting her feel as if she was alone. When she woke in the middle of the night she decided that she needed to tell her grandmother that she was going to meet with Jeff, she couldn't keep that from her. She hoped that she would agree that she could meet him alone, but she couldn't text or call her then as she probably would have been asleep.

Ally checked her phone for any new messages and sent a message explaining the meeting with Jeff to her grandmother. She also explained about the graffiti and that she wanted to ask Jeff about it. She waited anxiously for a reply but she received none.

Ally's heart fluttered nervously as she prepared herself some toast. Would he be as innocent as she hoped when she looked into his eyes? What if he wasn't? What if she only saw hatred in his demeanor? She shivered at the thought. Maybe a little coffee would help to clear her mind. She settled with her breakfast and tried to think of some questions that she wanted to ask him. She thought it would look pretty strange if she just sat there and stared at him for the entire visit.

Once Ally was finished with breakfast, she dressed, and said goodbye to Peaches and Arnold. She checked her phone again, but there was nothing from her grandmother. She tried to call her, but after a few rings it went to voicemail. She decided to drive by Freely Lakes on the way to the prison to see if she could speak to her.

Ally opened the front door and she was shocked to find Charlotte walking up the driveway.

Ally stared at her, too stunned to move.

"Ally." Charlotte walked towards her.

"Mee-Maw, what are you doing here?" Ally continued to stare at her.

"Jeff told me that you had an appointment with him today, when I spoke with him this morning." Charlotte shook her head. "So I got ready and started walking here. Then I received your text. But you are not going to see Jeff and that's that."

"But Mee-Maw..."

"Ally, I understand. You want to see if you believe him. But Jeff is important to me. I don't know exactly what that means yet, but I do know, I don't want the first time you meet him to be in a jail."

"I'm not going to judge him, Mee-Maw."

"He's embarrassed, Ally, and this will only make things worse. I'm asking you not to go."

Ally searched her eyes for a moment, then nodded.

"If you don't want me to, I won't. But I was hoping to get some more information from him."

"You leave that to me, sweetheart. And Ally?" She looked into her eyes.

"Yes?"

"I love you, and I know that you are only trying to protect me. You'll just have to trust me on this one."

"I do, Mee-Maw. And I love you, too."

"Okay, I need your car keys, please." Charlotte held out her hand.

"Here you go." Ally handed them over without an argument. She knew it would be useless.

"Do you need a lift to the shop?" Charlotte asked.

"No thanks, Mee-Maw, I'll walk."

Charlotte walked to Ally's car, and climbed in.

Ally watched as she backed out of the driveway. The moment she thought she had her grandmother figured out, was the same moment that she turned things completely around.

**

Charlotte drove towards the jail with one thing on her mind, information. Like Ally said she needed to get more information out of Jeff, things that he might not even realize were leads. But the moment that she pulled up to the tall prison walls all thoughts vanished from her mind. A heaviness landed in the pit of her stomach. She decided that the best thing to do was not to hesitate, thinking about it would make her feel worse. She opened up the car door and went straight to the prison entrance.

Charlotte went through security which she found surprisingly less involved than she thought it would be. She was guided to a room where she could have a few minutes to talk to Jeff. As she stepped inside she noticed that there were many other people there. Some sat alone, while others sat in pairs, and there was a low murmur in the room. She sat down at a table and waited. After a few minutes she wondered if he might have refused to see her. Then she saw him enter the room, escorted by a guard. When he sat down she knew he was surprised to see her.

"Hi, Jeff." She waited until he met her eyes to smile.

"Charlotte, I didn't want you to come to see me again, especially here." He sighed.

"I know, I'm sorry but I thought it was better that I visited you rather than Ally. And it's not really up to you where I go or who I see, now is it?" She searched his eyes. She reached across the table to touch his hand, but pulled back when she received a look from a guard.

"I guess you're right about that." He smiled in return. "I'm relieved that you talked Ally out of coming. I could only imagine the things that she'd say to me for putting you in this kind of position."

"I think she just wanted to look you in the eye. She can be a little overprotective. But her heart is in the right place."

"I can't imagine how it could be in any other place, with a wonderful woman like you who raised her."

"Enough of that." She waved her hand. "We don't have a lot of time, and we need to get down to business."

"All right then." He folded his hands and looked at her. "You're in charge."

"Exactly. Now, there are some questions I'd like you to answer for me."

"Anything." He nodded.

"Did you know about Dean having such a rough reputation?"

"Yes, I did. But that was in his past. I didn't think it would be a problem."

"So you were fine with being friends with him, throughout all of that?"

"I try not to be a person who judges. Honestly,

I met Dean after I met Bianca. When I met him, I thought maybe I needed to run as far as I could from Bianca and the rest of her family, as I didn't want to get in the middle of anything less than legal. But when I tried to break things off with her, she got very upset, she accused me of doing things that I didn't do. Dean paid me a visit, I think he meant to get revenge for his sister. But when I told him the truth, he believed me, and he apologized for his sister's behavior. We became friends after that, and even though I didn't always approve of his choices in life, he never tried to involve me in his business. It wasn't until he opened the jewelry store that we ever did any business together. I was very suspicious of him though, and it led to us having a few arguments over some deals. But during the short time that he was open I started to realize he was nothing but honest with me. He had his moments, Charlotte, but he wasn't a bad man, and he was a good friend to me. I would never do anything to hurt him." He closed his eyes and took a slow breath. "My heart breaks for his family. I can't even imagine what they must think of me right now."

"Is there anyone in their family that might not believe that you did this? Maybe we can gain their support for you?"

"I doubt it. I didn't know them well. The police are so determined it was me, and the evidence." He shook his head. "If only I'd made sure I had my ring sizer and mandrel with me when I left his shop, none of this would be happening. I never would have been there, my ring mandrel never would have been there."

"You can't focus on regret, Jeff. That won't get you anywhere. We need to find some way to prove that you weren't there when Dean was killed."

"There's nothing." He sighed. "I was in my car, a block away, maybe two. There's no way to prove that I wasn't at the shop."

"Okay, just take a breath. We're going to figure this out." She reached for his hand again, but the guard blew a short whistle. She sighed and rested her hand on the table instead.

"Charlotte, I appreciate all that you have done for me, but the truth is, there is no way to prove it."

"There's one way." She locked eyes with him.

"What's that?"

"We have to find the actual killer."

"If he did such a good job of covering his tracks that I am in jail, what makes you think that you'll be able to figure out who it is?"

"Because no one is perfect. He must have made a mistake somewhere along the way, we just have to figure out what it was."

"Charlotte, do you really believe I'm innocent?" He frowned.

"I know that you didn't do this, Jeff. But my opinion isn't going to change anything. It would help if you could think of anyone that Dean had a problem with. Anyone that might have held a grudge against him. Were you aware of the threats against him?"

"You mean the graffiti?" He narrowed his

eyes.

"Yes, I do. Why didn't Dean ever follow that up with the police?"

"Dean wasn't one to go to the police. The only reason he even reported it to the police, is because his daughter was working at the shop when it happened. He was worried for her, and she was frightened by it. But he never pushed them to look into it. He came from an old school way of life where a man handled his own problems."

"So how did he handle it?" Charlotte leaned forward some.

"He put the word out on the street that he wanted any information about the person who did it. He even offered a small reward. I tried to convince him that he should go through the police to make sure no one took advantage of him, but I guess his reputation prevented that."

"Did he ever get any information about who might have done it?"

"None. Not a word. He increased the reward,

and still nothing. Eventually he just let it go, since nothing new happened. But I know it still bothered him."

"I imagine it would. It's surprising that no one came forward with any information." She frowned.

"It surprised him, too. He was sure that someone should have known who did it. But like I said, he just let it go and tried to focus on other things."

"Interesting. I wish we could figure out who made the threat. Maybe whoever it was, is still holding a grudge."

"Maybe, but if they are, he didn't have any idea who they were. It's funny, I always expected for the truth to come out eventually, but it never did."

"I'll look into it and see if I can find anything out. In the meantime, try to stay positive, Jeff. I know that's not the easiest thing to do in your situation, but it might help."

"It will help." He nodded. "With your continued support, Charlotte, I feel a lot better."

"We're going to find a way to get all of this fixed."

"You might not be able to fix this, Charlotte. If you can't, you have to promise me that you'll let this all go and move on." He searched her gaze, his eyes filling with tears.

"There you go thinking you have some say in what I do again." She offered an affectionate smile. "Very soon, you're going to be free again, and I hope that when you are, we'll finally get to have that dinner that we planned with Ally and Luke."

"I hope so, too." He gazed into her eyes. "I have no idea what I did to get so lucky."

"Lucky? You think being imprisoned for a crime you didn't commit is lucky?" She stared at him.

"I think having an amazing woman like you care about me, is lucky, yes. It makes everything else a lot easier to tolerate."

"Soon, Jeff." She reached out to touch his cheek, but stopped as she recalled the rules of visitation.

"Soon." He nodded

Chapter Eleven

As Charlotte headed to the chocolate shop she thought back over everything that Jeff told her. Her mind fixated on the graffiti. Someone was upset enough with Dean to spray paint his building. That might be the best lead they had so far. She parked in the parking lot at the chocolate shop and noticed that there were no cars there. She stepped inside the shop and found Ally setting up for the day.

"Morning, Ally."

"Morning again." Ally turned to look at her. "How did it go?"

"I know he's innocent, Ally, but it's not going to be easy to figure out who did it." She filled her in about what she found out about the vandalism.

"Interesting," Ally said.

"I keep hoping that something will change, and Jeff will walk right out of that jail cell."

"It will, Mee-Maw, I know it will." Ally smiled.

"Okay, let's get to work." Charlotte brushed off her apron.

"I have a batch of chocolates to get out in the back, do you want to do it, or would you rather handle the counter?"

"The back if you don't mind. I'm not sure I'm ready to deal with people, yet. It's horrible going to a place like that." Charlotte met her eyes.

"Yes, it is. And to think that an innocent man can be behind bars for something he didn't do."

"Yes, I'm afraid that is a lot less surprising to me, but I have a few more years of experience than you." She patted Ally's shoulder, then stepped into the back. Ally wiped down the counter and checked on the displays. Although she paid attention to every detail, her focus was elsewhere. When her cell phone rang she was relieved to have a distraction.

"Hi Luke." She smiled at the sound of his voice.

"How did it go? I thought you were going to

text or call?"

"I'm sorry, I completely forgot. Actually, Mee-Maw stopped me from going. She visited Jeff instead."

"Oh? I guess I can understand that."

"You can?"

"Sure. She doesn't want you to have that impression of Jeff."

"That's what she said." Ally frowned. "She did find out a little more information."

"What kind of information?"

"She talked to him about the graffiti, and it turns out that Dean did a bit more investigating on his own."

"Oh really? Did he find anything?" His voice grew tense with anticipation.

"Unfortunately, no. He even put out a reward for anyone who gave him information. He was pretty surprised when he didn't get any responses. So, yet again, we have nothing to go on."

"Actually, that might be something."

"What might be?"

"Nothing."

"Luke." She sighed. "I don't understand."

"The fact that he got no responses after putting out a reward, is actually very telling. If anyone on the street knew who did it, that person would have come forward to collect the reward."

"So if no one came forward, then maybe no one on the street knew who did it." She nodded.

"Because, it wasn't someone on the street. It wasn't just some kid, or a random criminal."

"You mean it was someone that intentionally targeted Dean, someone Dean would never suspect."

"Yes, exactly. It doesn't narrow down our suspect pool by much, but it does give us something to look into."

"How do you plan to do that?"

"I'll go through the list of people we have as

having a connection to Dean and see if any have a history of vandalism. It's a long shot, but it might turn up something. I'll look into it right away."

"Thanks Luke. I really hope we can find something."

"Me too."

Ally hung up the phone and began to walk towards the back to update her grandmother. Before she could, the bell above the door rang out. In waltzed Mrs. Bing, Mrs. Cale and Mrs. White.

"Hello ladies." She smiled at them as they walked up to the counter. "I wondered if you would be in today."

"I heard rumors about a delicious new chocolate?" Mrs. Cale began to look through the sample trays.

"Oh yes, there are plenty to choose from." Ally gestured to the tray that held the new chocolates. "I'm looking forward to finding out how you like them."

"From what Mrs. White and Mrs. Bing have

said, I'm sure they will be delicious." She plucked a few from the tray, while Mrs. White and Mrs. Bing selected from the other trays. As they began to exclaim about how much they enjoyed the chocolates, Ally recalled that Mrs. White was involved in the same play that Chris was.

"Mrs. White, how is the play going?" She replaced some chocolates on the sample trays.

"Very well, thank you for asking, Ally. I'm quite happy to be taking part in it. The costumes, are amazing. You should come see one of the shows."

"I'd like to do that. I hear that Dean provided some of the jewelry." She caught Mrs. White's eye.

"Don't you mean Jeff?" She offered a light smile. "He is the one that made the beautiful jewelry, isn't he?"

"Yes, as far as I know." Ally frowned. "The order was supposed to go to another shop, Silvio's, but it was switched to Dean's at the last minute."

"Yes, I heard about that. Too bad for Silvio, and Troy. But the jewelry is flawless." Mrs. White swatted Mrs. Bing's hand away so that she could snatch one of the chocolates from the tray.

"Do you know Silvio and Troy?" Ally studied her. It shouldn't surprise her, as Mrs. White, Mrs. Cale, and Mrs. Bing, seemed to know everyone, both local and in the nearby towns.

"I don't know Silvio too well, but I do know Troy. I watched him grow up. He is from Broughdon, his parents were always putting him in the local sports and activities. I think they sensed even when he was young that there was something a little off about him." She sighed.

"Off?" Ally raised an eyebrow. "How so?"

"Oh you know, shy. He didn't ever seem to make friends easily and even though his parents encouraged him to be social, he always found ways out of it. He'd get hurt, or sick, or he would just refuse to participate. I think eventually his parents gave up, and then after that I didn't see much of him. It must have been lonely for him on that big farm though."

"Poor kid." Ally frowned. "I was pretty shy as a kid, too, and the last thing I would have wanted was to be forced into activities."

"I think they just wanted the best for him." Mrs. White shrugged. "Not every kid is going to be social. Living on a farm can make it more difficult."

"He grew up on a farm, hmm?" Ally smiled. "That must have been fun for him."

"Oh yes, Troy was always on the farm. It's a huge piece of land in Broughdon."

"Really? I didn't know that." Ally poured them each a cup of coffee to go with their chocolates. "Did he go to school around here, too?"

"No, he went to a private school in Broughdon. His parents always seemed like they were trying to give him the best. I don't know them well, but they seem like nice people."

"He was very polite to me. I can see why he does well as an assistant manager, making the deliveries and serving customers."

"It's nice to see that he finally has a job." Mrs. Cale rolled her eyes. "I can remember when he was getting fired left and right."

"When was that?" Ally added a few more pieces of chocolate to the sample tray.

"I guess he was just eighteen, or nineteen. He wasn't very reliable, according to the rumors I heard. He'd get a job, then fail to show up, or show up late. It took a little while for him to learn to be responsible I guess."

"Is he married?" Ally rested her hands on the counter. "I didn't notice a ring on his finger."

"No, not that I know of. In fact, I can't recall him ever dating any of the local girls. Maybe he dated someone in Broughdon though."

"Maybe." Ally nodded. "What about Silvio, are any of you familiar with him?"

"Oh Silvio." Mrs. Bing fluttered her eyelashes. "Now, he is quite dreamy."

"Stop it, he's not on the market." Mrs. White

wagged her finger at her.

"His wife lives in Florida!" Mrs. Bing huffed. "It's not as if they are really together."

"Interesting." Ally grinned. "So Silvio is a heart throb?"

"I wouldn't say that." Mrs. White shook her head.

"I would." Mrs. Bing giggled. "I've run into him a few times here in Blue River, and he always holds the door for me, he is so polite."

"Is he in Blue River often?" Ally listened intently.

"I think one of his favorite restaurants is here. I know I've seen him and Dean together for lunch at least once."

"Even though they were rivals?"

"I think it was before Dean opened up shop. You know, they used to be friends."

"They did?" Ally's eyes widened. "No, I didn't know that. How close were they?"

"I couldn't really say. I saw them together a few times in town. Once I saw Silvio and Dean at the diner, and another time I saw them walking through the park. They seemed chummy." She shrugged.

"Interesting. Silvio never mentioned them being friends." Ally narrowed her eyes. "Maybe I should speak to him again."

"Maybe you should." Mrs. Cale looked into her eyes. "I may not have known Dean well, but I'm certain the man didn't deserve to die. I'm also certain that Jeff didn't do this."

"I'm glad to hear that." Ally walked around the counter to join them. "I don't think he did this either. If any of you think of anything that might be helpful, please let me know."

"We will." Mrs. White took her hand. "I know this is a difficult time, but you really should come see the play. Maybe it can take your mind off things. Bring Charlotte, too."

"Thank you, I think we will do that if we get the chance. I'd love to see your work."

"I'd love for you to see it, too." Mrs. White nodded to the other women. "Let's go, ladies. I'm sure that Ally has other things to do."

"We'll be back to order chocolates!" Mrs. Bing waved over her shoulder as Mrs. Cale and Mrs. White escorted her towards the door. Ally had noticed that Mrs. Bing seemed to have had a change of heart about Jeff being guilty, or at least she made it seem that way in front of everyone.

Once they were gone, Ally replenished the samples.

"Are they gone?" Charlotte poked her head out of the kitchen.

"Yes, Mee-Maw. It's safe to come out."

"Oh, thank goodness. I thought they might never leave. I was just waiting for one of them to gossip about Jeff." Her cheeks flared as she stepped up next to Ally.

"Actually, it was the opposite. They all seemed very supportive of Jeff. In fact, thanks to them, I now know a lot more about Troy, and even Silvio

174

and Dean. Apparently, Silvio and Dean were once friends."

"Really? I didn't know that. I wonder if they had a falling out."

"I think they must have, as Silvio didn't mention their friendship." Ally rested her hands on the counter and stared out through the front window. "I really think there's something there we need to connect."

"I thought we decided that Silvio was too weak to kill Dean? Are you thinking differently now?"

"I'm not sure. I just have this feeling that we need to put two and two together. Maybe we should visit Silvio again?"

"That's not a bad idea."

"And also, I think we should pay a visit to the play. Maybe after we close today."

"I don't think it's open yet." Charlotte pulled out her phone. "I have it on my calendar as starting this weekend."

"I'm sure if they are about to open they are doing daily rehearsals. We can find our way in, and get a private showing." Ally tapped her fingertips on the counter. "I want to talk to Chris again. Maybe he knows something, and just doesn't realize that it's relevant."

"All right." Charlotte walked over to the register as a customer walked in. "Sounds like a plan."

For the rest of the day Ally and Charlotte switched between the register and the kitchen.

Ally lost herself in the process of making some chocolates, and for the first time since Jeff had been arrested, she felt herself relax. The smell, the texture, and the memories that both stirred within her, drew her back into a state of childlike wonder. It wasn't until she heard her grandmother's voice that she surfaced from it.

"Ally, I've already shut down the register. Do you need any help back there?"

"No, I'm okay, Mee-Maw. I'll be right out." Ally took off her apron and made sure everything was straightened up in the kitchen area. Then she put together a large sampler box of chocolates. When she met her grandmother in the front of the store, Charlotte already had the counters wiped down.

"I thought it might be nice to bring some chocolates with us when we crash the rehearsal," Ally said.

"Oh? So, you still think it's a good idea?"

"Absolutely. It's important to turn over every stone. Don't you think?"

"Yes."

"Now, let's go see a play."

Chapter Twelve

On the drive to the auditorium, Charlotte could barely sit still, she couldn't stop fidgeting.

"I just hope that Chris can tell us something," Charlotte said.

"The more I thought about it, the more I realized that seeing as he was one of the last people to see Dean alive, along with Jeff, and the killer, I really think he might have overlooked something, or saw something that he didn't even realize was evidence."

"Yes, that could definitely be possible. I bet he was in a rush, with all of the things he needed to arrange for the play."

"Let's just hope we can jog his memory." Ally pulled into the parking lot of the auditorium where the play was to be held. She noticed a line of cars parked near a side door. "That must be where they are rehearsing." She parked a space away from the last in the line of cars. After she stepped out, she waited for her grandmother to get out as well.

"What if they don't let us in, Ally?"

"We have the chocolates, remember?" Ally winked at her. "Nobody can turn down one of Charlotte's chocolates."

"Let's hope that holds true."

Ally led the way to the door, and noticed that it was propped open with a small block of wood. Carefully, to make sure that the wood remained in place, she opened the door, then stepped inside. Charlotte followed right after her. The auditorium was dark, aside from the lights up front near and above the stage. Several actors were engaged in a scene on the stage. Ally paused for a moment to take in the sight of the costumes and scenery designs. Were it not for the murder investigation she would be thrilled to have a preview of the play.

"Look, there are some seats up front." Ally guided Charlotte towards the front row of seats.

As they settled into the chairs, Chris turned to

look at them. After a second, a flicker of recognition softened the surprise in his expression.

Ally smiled in return and looked at her grandmother.

"I think he's fine with us watching."

As the play unfolded before her, Ally almost forgot about their purpose for being there. The actors were quite skilled at keeping her engrossed in the story.

"All right, that's enough for today." Chris clapped his hands. "Great job!"

"Bravo!" Charlotte clapped as well.

Ally joined in, and smiled at the actors as they left the stage.

A few came over to greet them, and Mrs. White popped up from behind the scenes.

"Charlotte, Ally, I didn't expect to see you here! I mean I know I told you to come and have a look but I didn't think you would so soon." She smiled at them. "Did you like what you saw so far?"

"Oh yes." Charlotte's eyes glowed as she described the scenes that she enjoyed the most.

Ally's attention turned towards Chris. She watched as he lifted up a few boxes and headed for the side door.

"Mee-Maw, I'm going to see if I can speak with Chris."

"Oh yes, I'll come with you." She said a quick goodbye to Mrs. White, then followed Ally to the door.

"Hi Chris." Ally paused beside his van.

"Hi." He smiled as he set the boxes inside, then turned to look at her. "It was nice of you two to come tonight."

"I hope it wasn't too distracting." Charlotte frowned.

"Not at all. It's always good to have an audience."

"We brought you these." Ally held out a box of chocolates for him. "For you and the actors."

"Just don't leave them alone with Mrs. White. You might not get any if you do." Charlotte grinned.

"I'll keep that in mind." He laughed. "Thank you so much for this. So be honest, what did you think?"

"The rehearsal looked great." Ally smiled. "We can't wait to see the finished product."

"We're still working out a few hiccups, but so far so good. It makes a big difference having the right decorations and props." He ruffled his hair. "It's quite a job."

"I know Mrs. White is thrilled to be part of it all." Ally slipped her hands into her pockets. "She's a very talented person."

"Yes, she is. Actually, she's the reason I switched my order to Dean's shop. That, and the price difference. She couldn't stop raving about Jeff's work, and once I saw it, I was convinced. He doesn't just make jewelry, he pays homage to the styles and techniques of the different eras. It allows me to keep our play authentic."

"I'm sure Jeff would be happy to hear that." Charlotte nodded with a small smile.

"Yes, sorry about the trouble he's in, I didn't realize that he was the one arrested for the crime when Ally called me to ask about Dean." He cleared his throat. "For what it's worth, I don't believe it for a second."

"You don't?" Charlotte's smile brightened.

"No. I've crossed paths with him a few times, and he was never anything but polite to me. Dean spoke very highly of him." He frowned. "It's still hard to believe that he's gone."

"You were one of the last people to see him. I'm sure he was happy that he could supply the things you needed for the play." Ally studied him. "Did he seem happy to you that day?"

"Sure." He shrugged. "I mean, I didn't notice anything strange. He did ask me not to mention who I switched my order to when I canceled my order with Silvio. I guess there had been some issues between them, and he didn't think it would be a good idea to stir things up."

"Interesting." Ally nodded. "So you canceled the order after you picked the items up from Dean?"

"Yes, actually, about an hour later. I got caught up in things and almost forgot."

"Who took the call when you canceled?" Ally held his gaze.

"Uh." He thought a moment, then nodded. "It was Silvio. I apologized, and asked if the items were already on their way to be delivered. He said no, that Troy was out on a delivery and he would let him know when he returned."

"How did Silvio sound?" Charlotte crossed her arms. "Was he upset about the canceled order?"

"If he was, he didn't let me hear it. In fact, he didn't sound surprised at all. It was almost as if he was expecting the call."

"Since so many people were going to Dean?" Ally pursed her lips. "He must have expected that you would switch, too."

"Maybe. But it wasn't quite like that. It really seemed like he already knew. He didn't argue with me, and he didn't even ask me who I'd switched my order to. Which seemed a little odd to me, as I had an entire excuse prepared as to why I couldn't tell him. Anyway, I guess there isn't anything we can do to change things now."

"What about Troy?" Charlotte tilted her head to the side. "Do you know him well?"

"Not too well. But what I do know of him, tells me he's a great guy."

"Why is that?" Ally smiled. "Sorry, I'm just curious because we might be getting some jewelry from him."

"I understand. Actually, Troy helped me out one day, when he could have given me a very hard time instead. That made a very big impression on me."

"Now I'm really curious." Ally grinned. "That sounds like a great story."

"It's not something I'm proud of,

unfortunately." He grimaced. "About a year ago, I discovered that there was an easy and quick way to get from Broughdon to Blue River. It involved trespassing on Troy's farm. At the time, I didn't think it was a big deal, what harm could it do? Then one rainy day, I didn't think about it, and drove right down the road on his property. It was very muddy and my car just sank right in. Troy was nice enough to tow me out. Not long after that they put a gate up though. I'm guessing they didn't want random people stranded on their farm." He shrugged and glanced over at Ally. "Never trust a dirt road."

"I'll keep that in mind." She smiled. "It was nice of Troy to help you out."

"Like I said, he seems like a stand-up guy. Thanks again for these chocolates."

"You're welcome, and thank you for giving us a little information about some people we might do business with."

"No problem. I hope that you'll get the chance to come see the play."

"I wouldn't miss it."

"Me neither." Charlotte offered a wide smile. "It had me on the edge of my seat, I can't wait to see what happens."

As Chris walked away, Ally looked over at her grandmother.

"It looks like we might have figured out how Troy could get from Blue River to Broughdon in less time."

"It's possible yes. But Chris also sang their praises."

"That's true, but remember how muddy the delivery van was?" Ally frowned.

"I do. But keep in mind that if these roads go through his farm, then he likely uses them all of the time. The van could have been muddy for several days before the murder took place."

"Yes, you're right."

"I say we take a drive and time it out though, what do you think?"

"On Troy's property?" Ally hesitated. "Like

Chris said, Troy and his family probably don't enjoy random people showing up on their property."

"I'll tell you what. We'll go by there, and if the gate is closed, we'll just keep driving. If it's open, we can check it out."

"Fair enough." Ally nodded.

Chapter Thirteen

Charlotte and Ally settled in the car. Ally searched on the phone for the address of Troy's property and then found it on a map. She waited until the map was up and then handed the phone to her grandmother.

"Interesting, Jen's shop is only shortly after the turn off to the farm."

"So Troy could have easily gotten to the shop and back with enough time to commit the murder."

"Maybe, let's drive it and find out." Charlotte pointed through the windshield at the road ahead of them. "Go left."

Ally drove in the direction her grandmother instructed.

"We need to get a good idea of how long it would take Troy to make those deliveries if he used those back roads. If it cuts enough time off it opens him up as a suspect, along with Silvio."

"Do you think they could have worked together?" Charlotte glanced up from the map on her phone. "Maybe to protect their business?"

"It seems like a huge step to me to murder someone over competition, but I'm sure it wouldn't be the first time."

"At that next light, I think we go right and then down about three miles."

"Great." Ally turned in the direction that her grandmother directed. As she turned on to the new road, she noticed that there were far fewer houses and buildings. The further down she drove, the more sparse it became. Flat land stretched out on either side, with no hint of houses in any direction. A small road opened out on to the main road. Several feet back from the turn was a metal gate.

"That must be the new gate that Chris mentioned, and it's closed." Charlotte sighed.

"But it might not be locked." Ally glanced over at her.

"That's true." Charlotte looked back at the gate. "I don't see any lock."

"Let's just check."

Ally crept the car up to the gate. Then she climbed out of the car. When she reached the gate she noticed a deep groove in the dirt road from the gate being swung back and forth. For the gate to be quite new, and the groove to be so deep, she was sure that it was used very often. When she tried the gate, it swung open easily. Once she was back in the car, she drove through the gate.

"Mee-Maw, what if we get stuck?"

"It hasn't rained for a little while, so hopefully there won't be too much mud left. Just take it slow, and we'll keep a look out for any big dips."

Ally inched her way along the road. She couldn't help but notice the beauty of their surroundings. The further along the road they drove the more trees cropped up around them, and soon she knew that it would be impossible to be spotted from the road. She slowed to a stop when she arrived at a fork in the road.

"Which way?" She frowned.

"I don't know, the GPS stopped working. I guess there isn't much service out here."

"It looks like that road is well used." Ally pointed out the road that went to the right.

"Let's try it." Charlotte nodded.

Ally steered the car down the narrow road. The further along they got, the more bumpy the road grew. Even though there weren't any big puddles, the dirt road was thick with mud and she wasn't feeling confident that the car wouldn't get stuck.

"We'd better be ready to push." She stepped on the gas a little more.

"Don't worry, I think we'll make it, the road looks a bit drier up there. Oh and look, the GPS came back on." She held out her phone for Ally to see. "We're only ten minutes away from the store now."

"Wow, that's incredible. Cutting through the farm cut the travel time in at least half."

"This changes things. Troy could have easily doubled-back and taken over the store while Silvio committed the crime."

"Or he could have done it himself." Ally tilted her head towards the highway as they turned on to it. "After all Troy is familiar with the roads on his family's farm. He is also stronger than Silvio and more capable of committing the murder "

"That's true." Charlotte frowned. "But would he really have a motive?"

"I'm not sure. We'll have to look into it more. We know that Dean was poaching Silvio's customers."

"But, Troy doesn't own the business, would it really bother him that much to lose customers? He's just an assistant manager."

"That's true. Maybe there was something more going on between Troy and Dean that we don't know about." She pulled into the parking lot of the shop. It was still closed, with no sign of anyone else around. However as she parked, she noticed some movement through the front window. "Mee-Maw, someone is in there!"

"Ally, get down. Whoever it is, we don't want them to know that we spotted them." Charlotte slouched down in her seat.

"I'm going to go around the back and see if I can find out who is inside." Ally already had her door open, and slid out on to the pavement.

"Ally!" Charlotte hissed and tried to grab for her hand.

"Don't worry, Mee-Maw, I won't let myself be seen." She continued to creep across the parking lot, with her head low, and her eyes on the front window of the shop. If the person inside spotted her, he showed no sign of it.

As she rounded the corner of the shop, her knees were relieved to feel the transition from pavement to soil. She picked her way carefully through the low grass until she reached the rear of the shop. When she peered around the back corner, she noticed that there was a car close to the back door. Although it wasn't paved, and there were no parking spots there, someone had decided to use it as a parking lot. She didn't recognize who the car belonged to, but it did look familiar to her.

She crept up to the back of the car and pulled out her phone to take a picture of the license plate. As far as she knew there shouldn't be anyone at the shop, and it was clear that whoever it was had gone to great lengths to hide their car. She saw the back door was propped open as she made her way around the car. As she moved she did her best to stay out of sight. When she reached the back door, she noticed a shadow as it moved past. She held her breath and wondered if she was about to get caught. There was no time to run for cover, so she froze, and waited to see if the man inside the building would discover her.

"Look, I'm just trying to get whatever we can salvage. If that old man thought I was taking over his business, he was crazy. The sooner we can sell the place, the sooner we can get out of this town." He paused.

She realized that he must be speaking on the

phone.

"She'll come around. If she doesn't, oh well, at least we don't have kids yet. The old man was so traditional that he passed the business down to me, not his daughter, so she has no ground to stand on."

Ally cringed as she overheard the terrible way that he spoke about Erica. It angered her to think that Dean left his business to a son-in-law who appeared to have no regard for his wife's feelings. If Brad knew that Dean left the business to him, that might have motivated him to kill Dean. Maybe Brad had fallen on hard times, and he decided he could make things better by inheriting and selling the business. No matter what his plan, it wasn't a positive one for Erica. She started to draw back from the door, but Brad suddenly swung it open. He was about to step out, when Ally heard a horn blare from the front of the shop. She knew it had to be her grandmother.

***

It wasn't hard for Charlotte to tell that the

man inside the shop had headed to the back. Once a cloud moved over the sun there wasn't such a glare on the front windows and she was able to make out his figure as he moved around inside. He didn't seem to be trying to keep himself hidden. When she saw him walk into the back, her heart lurched in her chest. She was sure that wherever Ally was she was in danger of being caught. The only thing she could think to do was blare the horn in an attempt to distract the man from Ally. It seemed to work as a few seconds after the horn sounded he opened the front door of the shop.

"What do you want?" He peered through the sun which had grown brighter since the cloud moved aside. "Who are you?"

Charlotte wasn't surprised to see it was Brad and she knew that the moment he discovered who she was he wouldn't be pleased. He had lost his temper with her once already. What excuse could she give him for being at the closed shop? Reluctantly, she stepped out of the car.

"I'm sorry to bother you, but I really need to get a look inside the shop."

"What could you possibly need to look at inside the shop?" He took a step forward, then he narrowed his eyes as he recognized her. "You again? I think this could be considered harassment."

"Please, you have to understand. I left a ring in the shop with Dean that he was supposed to re-size. I just need to get it back. I'll sign whatever papers you want me to sign. I just need the ring back. It's a family heirloom."

"I'm sure that's what you want. If there was a ring in the shop that belonged to you then why didn't I know about it? Why didn't you say something before?" He crossed his arms.

"I tried to, but you wouldn't let me talk. You threw me out of your house, don't you remember?"

"Because you're the girlfriend of the man that murdered my father-in-law."

"Allegedly." She locked her eyes to his. "That hasn't been proven."

"I think if he's in handcuffs then there's a pretty good chance that it's true."

"You can believe what you want about him, but that doesn't change the fact that Dean was in possession of something that belonged to me, and I would like it back. Now, I could go to the police about it, but I thought we could just have a friendly exchange. As I said, I'm willing to sign any paperwork that you need me to. Since it's obvious you're not planning on reopening the shop, then I need to get it now, before it disappears."

"I'm not sure what makes you think I'm not going to reopen the shop. My father-in-law left it to me."

"The boxes." She tilted her head towards a stack of boxes that she could clearly see through the large front window. "If you were planning on keeping the store open, you wouldn't be boxing everything up."

"I can do whatever I please with what is in the shop." He shrugged. "Maybe instead of trying to get in the middle of other people's business, you should ask yourself why you are so meddlesome. Is there something missing from your life that you have to create so much drama?"

"I'll thank you to watch your tone, young man. Have you no respect for your elders?"

"I only respect those who have earned it."

"And had Dean earned your respect?"

His jaw rippled as he studied her. "Of course. He was my wife's father."

"Would he approve of you holding someone's jewelry hostage?"

"All right fine." He sighed and stepped away from the door. "Come in, and make it quick. I have things to get done."

Charlotte stepped into the shop, and took a breath as she recognized that it was the last place that Dean was alive. She had actually never been inside the shop before, and found that it looked very similar to Silvio's. Although, there were a few more display cases and stock, everything was positioned in a similar way. She wondered if Dean modeled his shop after Silvio's.

"All of the jewelry in the shop is in the display case. If your ring isn't there, then I have no idea where it might be." He walked over to a stack of boxes and began to tape the top one shut.

"Does Erica know that you're packing up her father's shop?"

"My wife is beside herself with grief. She doesn't need to be distracted from that by the mundane things that need to be done."

"I just thought she might want to continue to run the shop, in honor of her father."

"No." He narrowed his eyes. "Is your ring there, or not?"

"I'm looking." Charlotte jumped when she heard a thump in the back of the shop.

"What was that?" He dropped the tape gun on top of the box and turned to face Charlotte.

Charlotte held her breath, as she was sure the sound must have been caused by Ally.

***

Ally grabbed the can of paint she'd knocked over and set it upright again. As quiet as she'd tried to be, she still managed to walk into something. It was fairly easy to do as the storage room she'd slipped into was packed from floor to ceiling with junk. There was no organization to it, and though some of the items could be associated with the shop, many seemed to be personal in nature. Dean was a bit of a pack rat, it seemed. She froze as she waited to see if Brad would come to investigate the sound.

Ally knew that her grandmother was in the shop, as she could hear her voice. She heard Brad exclaim about the sound. With only moments to spare before he would discover her, she had to find a place to hide. There was a pile of boxes pushed up against a shelf in the back of the storage room. She managed to squeeze behind the boxes and crouch down beneath the bottom shelf.

With a deep breath she tried not to think about what might be under there with her, hidden in the dust and the cobwebs. Was that a spider crawling in her hair? She clenched her teeth and waited for the inevitable. How would he react when he found her there? She heard heavy footsteps approach the storage room.

"Is there someone in there?" He stood at the entrance of the room. "Tell me now, before I get my gun."

Ally's eyes widened. She held her breath.

"Brad? Brad!" Charlotte followed him towards the back of the store. "I really don't have time for this. Can you please help me with my ring? I have a meeting I need to get to."

"A meeting?" He turned to look at her. "I think there's someone burglarizing my shop and you're more concerned about a meeting?"

"Oh dear, you think someone is trying to rob you?" Charlotte clutched her purse. "Let's take a look." She pushed past him into the entrance of the storage area. "It was probably just a rat. I see some droppings right there."

"Droppings?" He took a step into the room. "That's just dirt."

"Are you sure? Rat droppings can easily look like dirt."

"There are no rats in my shop."

"How do you know that? It's only been your shop for a short time. Have you even gone through everything that's in this room?"

"No, of course not, because I got interrupted by you." He narrowed his eyes. "Did you find your ring?"

"I think so, but I need a closer look to be sure that it is the right one."

"All right, let's take a look." He followed her back to the front of the shop.

She pointed out a ring through the thick glass. "It looks like that one, but the glass is so dirty it's hard to be sure."

"The glass is not that dirty." He shook his head and opened the sliding door on the back of the shelf.

As he pulled out the ring she pointed out, Charlotte stole a glance towards the back hallway. She hoped that Ally would take the opportunity and get out before Brad got any more suspicious.

"Is this it?" He held up the ring.

"No, I'm sorry that's not it. It looks similar, but that's not it. Are you sure you don't have any more jewelry somewhere in the shop?"

"No, this is it. Are you sure that Dean had your ring?"

"I suppose it's possible that he gave it back to my granddaughter, Ally. I'll have to ask her about it."

"That might have been something to do before you came here and disrupted my day." He rolled his eyes and placed the ring back in the display case. "Do find out, as I'm sure that Dean would have left some kind of record of the ring."

"You may be right. Dean was always reliable that way."

"Hm." He locked eyes with her for a moment. "There's not a single thing about you that I trust. Please leave."

She stared back at him for a moment. "I'm sorry that you feel that way. I'm a very trustworthy person."

"The door is that way." He pointed to it.

"It's probably a good thing that you're closing the shop as you don't seem to have the personality to interact with customers."

"You know nothing about my personality, lady." He shook his head and started to walk back towards the storage area.

***

Ally inched her way out from under the shelf, and did her best not to knock anything else over in the process. Just when she thought she was clear, she discovered that there was yet another problem. The door to the storage room was now shut, and she wasn't sure that she could open it without making a sound. She grabbed a cloth that looked a bit like a handkerchief from a nearby pile of junk and used it to turn the knob as slowly as she could. Once she pulled the door open she looked up and down the hallway. She could hear her grandmother still speaking to Brad, which was a relief, but she knew she didn't have much time to get out. Once she made it into the hallway she headed straight out the back door. The moment she made it out, she looked back over her shoulder, and caught sight of Brad headed for the storage room. She hurried around the corner of the building, and saw Charlotte drive the car towards the edge of the parking lot. She jumped right into the passenger side and breathed a sigh of relief.

"Wow, that was close."

"I'll say, what were you thinking?" Charlotte shook her head.

"Me? You're the one that went inside the shop."

"So did you." She raised an eyebrow. "Or was that someone else's foot that I saw peeking out from underneath that shelf?"

"You saw me?" Her eyes widened.

"I did, but Brad didn't. What were you doing in there?"

"I just wanted a chance to get inside. I thought maybe, just maybe there would be some shred of evidence that would give us a direction to go in."

"And did it?" Charlotte glanced over at her.

"Unfortunately, no. The only thing I came out with is this." She held up the handkerchief to show her grandmother. "It's not exactly going to solve any crimes."

"Maybe not." Charlotte laughed. "Is it clean at least?"

"I hope so." Ally looked at the handkerchief again, then froze. "Mee-Maw, there's initials on it."

"Initials?"

"TC." She looked over at her grandmother. "Troy Culpepper?"

"Oh, wow. That's possible. But it could be someone else's initials right?"

"It could be, but this was laying right on top of one of the boxes. If it does belong to Troy, I don't think it should have been in there. Maybe when Dean was killed, Troy came in through the back, and hid in the storage room."

"Maybe. The police probably wouldn't have noticed it in that overstuffed storage area." She frowned. "I think it could be a good clue. I wonder if Luke could get some evidence off it to prove that it belongs to Troy?"

"I'll text him." Ally pulled out her phone and sent a text, along with a picture of the handkerchief to Luke. "Hopefully, he'll find something. From what we've learned about Troy, he did seem to have some issues. Maybe he had a problem with Dean that we don't know about."

"Yes, maybe he did. Now that we know how fast he could have gotten back here, I think we definitely need to consider him. Now, I'd like to go home and rest."

"Sure, we're almost there."

"No, I mean to Freely Lakes. If you don't mind, Ally, I need a little time to myself this evening."

"No, I don't mind. I understand."

"And don't forget about Arnold's appointment tomorrow. It is an early appointment so we can make it back in time to open the store."

"I can go in and get things started at the store if you would rather take Arnold yourself."

"No, I'd like you to be there. You haven't met the vet, and I want to get your opinion of her. I'm not so sure she's the right fit. She doesn't seem very fond of pigs."

"Not fond of Arnold? How is that even possible?" Ally laughed. "Sure, no problem. Arnold and I will pick you up in the morning."

She pulled into the parking lot of Freely Lakes and gave Charlotte a kiss on the cheek.

"Perfect, see you in the morning."

Ally waited to be sure that her grandmother got inside, then headed back towards the cottage. It still felt a little strange to her to be living there without her grandmother, but she knew it was best for both of them.

As soon as she was settled on the couch she breathed a sigh of exhaustion. It had been a close call at Dean's shop, and her heart still pounded from it. As she began to relax from the day, her cell phone rang. She checked and saw that it was Luke.

"Hi, just who I was hoping to hear from."

"I'm glad you feel that way, because I have some bad news for you."

"Oh no, what?"

"There's no way we're going to get anything we can use off that handkerchief, and even if we did, it's not going to place Troy at the scene."

"Why not?" She frowned. "I found it in the storage room at Dean's shop."

"Right, but it's not there now. Your word isn't

enough to place it there."

"Great." She ran her hand across her forehead. "So it is useless."

"Not entirely, even though we can't get evidence off it, we can assume that it does belong to Troy, and that if you found it in that storage room, then he was there at some point, and likely recently. It may not prove anything, but it certainly gives us a direction to go in."

"That's good at least." She breathed a sigh of relief. "So, do you think it could have been Troy?"

"I'm reserving judgment on this until I get more information."

"Always the logical thinker."

"And, how exactly did you end up in the storage room in Dean's shop?"

"Uh, that's kind of a long story."

"I'm sure it is." He sighed. "And I'm sure you're too tired to tell me tonight. What is your day like tomorrow? Can we get some time together?"

"Sure. I have to take Arnold to the appointment with the vet in the morning, then the shop, but by dinner time I should be free. Want to come over and I'll cook?"

"No, let's go out. I don't want you to have to cook after working all day."

"I don't really consider making chocolates work."

"Well, it is, and you need to be able to have a little fun, too. Where would you like to go?"

"Surprise me."

"All right." He laughed again. "Goodnight Ally, try to get some rest."

"I will, thanks. Good night, Luke." She hung up the phone, then stretched out on the couch. As tired as she was, she doubted she would be awake for much longer. The thought of going out to dinner with Luke gave her something to look forward to.

Chapter Fourteen

The next morning Ally woke up a little early. She made sure Arnold had plenty to eat and that his snout was clean. Arnold snorted happily as she put on his harness and leash. Once Peaches had her breakfast, Ally and Arnold headed out to the car. She put down his blanket in the backseat along with one of his favorite toys. He curled up on the seat and yawned.

"Oh, sorry to disturb your beauty sleep." Ally grinned. She started the car and drove in the direction of Freely Lakes. When she pulled up she grabbed her phone to text her grandmother, but before she could Charlotte stepped out through the door.

"Were you waiting for me?" Ally popped open the door for her.

"Maybe. I'm a little nervous about Arnold's appointment."

"Why? He seems very happy and healthy."

"I know, but I just wonder if he's getting enough exercise."

"I do take him on walks."

"True, but Arnold has always been a runner. Once in a while I would take him to the dog park to let him run, but then a few of the dog owners got a little upset because he spooked some of their dogs." She rolled her eyes. "He's just a little pig, but so very scary apparently."

"Aw, that's too bad. Maybe I'll try taking him again sometime. If anyone tries to chase us off, I'll just tell them he's a hairless dog."

Arnold snorted from the backseat.

"I think he's offended." Charlotte laughed.

"Sorry Arnold." Ally glanced at him in the rearview mirror.

He snorted again, then rested his head on his blanket.

"Did you get any sleep last night?" Charlotte glanced over at her.

"Some."

"I didn't." Charlotte sighed. "I keep thinking about Jeff in jail."

"I know it must be hard, Mee-Maw."

"What else can we do? I feel like we've hit a dead end."

"There is one more thing we can do, Mee-Maw. We can take another look around the outside of the store. If we believe that Troy may have had something to do with this, and that he was hiding out in the storage room, then he probably took the same path I did to get into the storage room. Or maybe Troy wasn't involved, but the killer might have still hid out in the storage room. We can search the ground around the outside of the store and see if there was anything left behind. It's a long shot, but it's worth a look, don't you think?"

"I think so. I don't know what else we can do. I feel so helpless, knowing that Jeff isn't the killer, and yet he's likely going to trial for it."

"Not if we can stop it." She patted the back of her grandmother's hand. "We're not done yet,

Mee-Maw." She glanced at her watch. "We still have a half hour before Arnold's appointment. We can pass by the shop right on our way to it. Why don't we just go on the way?"

"All right, that sounds good." Charlotte looked over her shoulder at Arnold. "Want to go for a longer ride, buddy?" She rubbed the top of his head. "We can let him get a little exercise before the appointment, too, maybe he'll be calmer for it then."

Arnold snorted happily.

"He misses you." Ally grinned. "Sometimes I think he is wandering around the house looking for you. Then you come over, and he's thrilled."

"I miss him, too. Especially his snoring. It's hard to fall asleep without it."

"Seriously?" Ally laughed. "When he insists on sleeping in the bedroom with me I have to wear ear plugs!"

"You get used to it." Charlotte leaned back over the seat and stroked his ear fondly. "At least

I did. So what do you think we'll find at the shop?"

"I don't know, maybe just something that the police overlooked? I find it hard to believe that a murder could be committed without a single trace of evidence."

"Yes, so do I. But it seems this murder was committed and all the wrong evidence was left behind."

"We do know that it's possible Troy made his way back to the shop by using the back roads that run through his farm."

"That's true, but we have no way to prove it. And even if he did make it back, there's still no evidence that we can use that he was ever even at the shop."

"And we still haven't found another possible murder weapon."

"Don't remind me." Charlotte sighed. "I hope we'll be able to find something."

"Here we are." Ally parked in front of the shop. It was dark, with no sign of anyone being there recently. "Great, it looks like Brad isn't around today."

"Good, Arnold can have a walk around." She opened the back door and grabbed Arnold's leash as she guided him down off the back seat, and out the door onto the sidewalk.

"I doubt we'll find any footprints, since it's been so long since the crime. But maybe the murderer was in a rush and left something behind."

"All right, I'll start over here, by the parking lot, you start by the building."

Ally began to walk along the edge of the building. She searched the dirt for anything that might be out of the ordinary. She looked at the brick wall for any sign of clothing or marks that might have been left behind. When she came up empty, she even got down on her knees and began to look through the grass and dirt. She was peering at a piece of plastic between two blades of grass, when she heard Arnold squeal and snort.

"Arnold, stop that!" Charlotte grunted as she

tried to control him with the leash. "Come back here!"

No matter how hard she tugged, he pulled at the harness until he made it a few steps closer to the dumpster.

"Don't let him get into the trash, Mee-Maw! If we leave a mess behind, Brad will point his finger at us first."

"It's not as if I'm trying to!" She huffed.

Arnold lunged forward and went straight for the dumpster. Instead of stopping near the trash, he began to dig in the dirt on one side of the dumpster.

"Arnold!" Ally grabbed his leash that was still in her grandmother's hand and tried to pull him away from the dirt. "What in the world are you looking for?"

"Wait, Ally, let him go. Maybe he saw something that we didn't."

"All right." Ally glanced up. "Did you hear a car?"

"A car? How can you hear anything over Arnold's squealing?"

"Let's see what you found, boy." Ally crouched down beside him and peered into the dirt. "Mee-Maw! It's something metal." She brushed the dirt aside, and discovered a long cylinder shaped metal object. The more dirt she brushed away, the more familiar the object looked. As she realized what it was, she gasped. "Mee-Maw, it's a..."

"A ring mandrel." The voice came from just behind her. Ally jumped to her feet and spun around to find Troy just a step away. Instant fear flooded through her body. There was no question in her mind now that Troy was the killer, and there he was, just a breath away from her.

"Mee-Maw! Run!" Ally moved in front of her.

"No, don't do that." Troy cleared his throat and Ally noticed the small knife in his hand for the first time. It was mostly concealed against his leg. "We don't want this to get messy, do we?" He looked between the two of them.

"Troy, put the knife down." Charlotte stared

at him. "You're not going to use it."

"What I will do and won't do, that's for me to decide." His eyes grew cold. "Now please, hand me the mandrel, Ally."

Ally's hand shook as she reached back down into the dirt to pull it out. "Troy, we don't even know if this is yours. I mean, the police won't be able to tell."

"I think they will, since it's engraved. A gift from Silvio when he made me assistant manager. I was so proud, when he gave me that. He even had the cleaning cloth embroidered with my initials. Little did I know that his kindness would turn out to be a huge risk for me. Give it to me please." He held his free hand out. Ally placed the mandrel in his palm, and drew her hand back fast. Her eyes fixated on the knife for several seconds before she blinked and forced herself to look away. Troy had no reason to keep them alive, so she believed the only chance for their survival was to keep him talking. Maybe someone on the street would notice their plight.

"Phones on the ground, ladies, and don't try to tell me you don't have one, I know you both do."

Charlotte and Ally reluctantly tossed their phones down on the ground.

Arnold sniffed them with interest.

"You killed Dean?" Charlotte studied him. "But why? What did he do to you that would turn you into a murderer?"

"What did he do?" He chuckled. "All my life, I failed at everything." He shrugged. "School wasn't my cup of tea, as my mother would say. I couldn't hold down a job. My personality conflicted with people, that's the polite way they put it. Then, Silvio hired me. He took the time to really teach me step by step about the costume jewelry supply business. He didn't judge me, he didn't throw me out like the rest. Instead he taught me how to deal with my anxiety and turn it into something good. Then he even promoted me. Finally, I was in charge of something, and not constantly waiting for the ax to drop."

"And then Dean's shop threatened to put

Silvio's out of business." Charlotte supplied, as her heart pounded. "But you have to understand that was just business. It wasn't personal."

"Oh, it was certainly personal. Dean set his sights on Silvio and was determined to destroy him. Silvio spoke to him about it, they argued and had a falling out, but Silvio didn't do enough. I had to take care of the problem. I mean I tried to be reasonable. I tried to talk to him about it. Every time he stole one of our customers, I would call him and try to reason with him. Dean would play me, as if he understood, and then just steal another customer."

"You called Dean shortly before he was killed? What did he say to you that made you decide to do this?" Ally locked eyes with him.

"He laughed at me. He told me to stop calling him and start paying more attention to my customers, then maybe I would still have some. But what he didn't know was that Silvio was counting on Chris' account to keep the store afloat. When we lost him, I knew Silvio was going to close the shop. I couldn't let that happen. I knew if Dean wasn't around then it would go back to the way it was before Dean opened his shop and all of the customers would go back to Silvio. I decided I would go talk to him, one more time."

"But it didn't go well." Ally looked at the knife again. "Troy, you were under emotional and psychological stress. A jury will understand that. But they won't understand you harming two innocent women. Just let us go, and you'll have a chance of getting out of all of this."

"Oh, will I?" He laughed. "Do you think Silvio will forgive me for this? He hated Dean, but he didn't have the strength or the courage to do anything about it. I went to talk to Dean again. I knew that if I went in the front door he would throw me out. So I went in through the back. I heard him on the phone with someone, mocking me, mocking Silvio. He said he was going to take out a restraining order against me to keep me away from the shop. I knew then, that if I didn't do something, he was going to ruin my life. So I did the one thing I could do for Silvio. I was brave enough, and strong enough to do it. All I had with me was my ring mandrel. But it worked." He stared down at it in the palm of his hand. "I thought it was fitting that his gift to me, helped to provide my gift to him."

"You killed a man over a little competition." Charlotte narrowed her eyes. "There was no reason to murder him."

"I had to. Silvio was going to lose everything. He wouldn't listen to reason. Even when I…"

"You mean, you were going to lose everything." Ally gritted her teeth. "This was never really about Silvio."

"I guess you could say that." He shrugged. "Either way, Dean was the problem. When I confronted him, I gave him one last chance. I told him to give us back Chris' account. But he didn't. Instead he was rude, called me names, told me that Silvio was going to fire me anyway. I got so angry, I just couldn't stop myself. I pulled out my ring mandrel, and that was it." He closed his eyes.

"I thought, it couldn't possibly kill him. But it did. I had to get out of there fast, and I didn't want to take the mandrel with me in case the police stopped me. So I cleaned mine and the one near the body hoping the police might presume that that one was the murder weapon. Which they did." He smiled. "I almost threw my mandrel into the dumpster, but I realized that the police would search there for evidence. So I buried it instead. I meant to come back here and get it, but every time I had the chance the police were here, or Brad, or you. And now, this." He shook his head. "So you see, I have no choice but to protect myself. Just like Dean, you put yourselves in this position. It's not my fault, it's yours."

"You don't have to do that, Troy." Ally tried to catch his eyes. "You can let us go. You made a mistake, in the heat of the moment. The police will understand and you can get a good lawyer."

"No!" He screamed the word. "I am not going to spend the rest of my life in jail. I will not let that happen."

"Then you are going to murder us, Troy? Two innocent women? I don't believe you have it in you. You killed Dean because you were angry at him, because he insulted you and his actions threatened to take everything from you. We're not doing that," Charlotte said.

"You might not be doing it, but if I let you live, my life will be over. So really, it is self-defense."

"There's no way you can get away with this." Ally shook her head. "You're out in the open here, one scream will get the attention of everyone in the neighborhood."

"Go ahead." He chuckled. "No one's listening. Their doors are closed, their windows are locked, and their air conditioning is on. But you're right. It would be better if we had some privacy. Both of you need to get into the delivery truck, we'll handle this somewhere else."

"There's no way we're getting in that van." Charlotte glared at him.

"No?" He slid the ring mandrel into his pocket, then grabbed Ally around the chest and

228

pinned her arms down beneath his arm. "I've killed once already, you don't think I can again?" He rested the knife against the side of Ally's neck. Ally started to squirm, then froze when she felt the cool metal on her skin. She let Arnold's leash slip from her hand. She had no idea what Troy might do to the pig, and hoped that he would be safer on his own. The moment he sensed freedom, he took off with a snort.

"Okay, all right, Troy. Just calm down. We'll get into the van." Charlotte held up her hands in front of her. "Just lower that knife and we'll do whatever you want."

"I thought you might change your mind." He lowered the knife back to his side, then tilted his head towards the delivery van parked at the end of the sidewalk. "Let's go." Charlotte walked ahead of them to the van, while Troy kept his grip tight around Ally.

"Troy, just let us go. You're not a murderer. You got upset in the moment, you were trying to protect yourself and Silvio. Do you really want the deaths of two women on your shoulders?" Ally pleaded with him.

"I didn't want any of this, Ally, but the easiest way to take care of this problem is to get rid of both of you. Open the door." He locked eyes with Charlotte. "And get inside."

Ally watched her grandmother slide open the door and put one foot up into the van. Charlotte glanced back at Ally with a grimace.

"Get in, I said," Troy growled his words.

"All right, I'm getting in." Charlotte pulled her other foot up into the van. Behind her, she heard Ally grunt as Troy pushed her towards the van.

"There's still time to let us go, Troy. Just think about what you're doing here." Ally's voice wavered with desperation.

"I'm thinking just fine, and this is the best solution." He pushed Ally into the van behind her grandmother, then slammed the door shut behind her. Ally crawled across the van to her grandmother and wrapped her arms around her.

"Are you okay?"

"Yes, I'm fine. Are you?" Her eyes locked to Ally's. "Did he hurt you?"

"No, but we have to get out of here, Mee-Maw. He's crazy."

"I know." Charlotte looked towards the front of the van as Troy climbed inside and started the engine. She had no idea where he might be taking them. "I hope that Arnold is okay."

"I'm sure he will be."

"The sooner we can get to him the better."

"We can try to jump out."

"No, he's going too fast. Let's just think this through. Will Luke be looking for you?"

"No, not until later. He thinks I'm at the vet appointment with Arnold."

"Okay, then we're in this alone. Maybe we can find a way to distract him."

"How?" Ally looked towards the front of the van. "Should I try to attack him?"

"He might flip the van as fast as he's going. I don't know if that's the best idea."

"He could be taking us back to his farm. Once he gets us out there, no one will ever find us, Mee-Maw. We can't let him get that far."

"I agree. If we have to, we'll attack, but let's try to think of something else first."

"Mee-Maw, he's already killed, he'll have no problem killing us, too."

Abruptly the van slowed down

"We're slowing down." Charlotte gripped the side of the van. "There must be traffic."

"We should try to get out now." Ally reached for the rear door.

"No Ally, not yet. If we roll out even at this speed the car behind us won't have time to stop. But maybe we can signal to someone behind us to call for help."

"Yes, that's a good idea." Ally leaned up close to the back window and peered over the edge. She knew that if she lifted her head too high, Troy might notice her by the back door. "Look, Mee-Maw," Ally whispered to her grandmother as she pointed through the window.

Charlotte eased up on to her knees to peek outside. There, in the middle of traffic, was Arnold. His little legs struggled to keep up with the van as his leash flew through the air. Behind him a few cars beeped their horns.

"My little hero, he's trying to save us!" Charlotte exclaimed. "I hope he doesn't get hurt."

"I hope so." Ally grimaced as her heart started pounding at the thought of Arnold being in danger.

"Someone might spot us because of him. When the van comes to a stop the next time, at a light, whatever, we have to get out," Charlotte whispered, and shot a glance in the direction of the front of the van.

"Mee-Maw, what if we can't get out and he catches us? He might just decide to kill us on the spot."

"He's not going to let us go, Ally. And no one knows that we were stopping by the shop. It will be hours before anyone even realizes that we're missing. Jumping out is going to be our only chance. I know it's scary, but I can't think of another way."

"You're right." Ally nodded. "We just have to be brave."

"Quiet back there!" Troy shouted from the driver's seat.

Ally put her finger to her lips.

Charlotte nodded and grasped her granddaughter's hand. Now it was only a matter of time before they would have to decide to jump, or risk disappearing on Troy's farm.

Chapter Fifteen

Luke stepped out of the police station and headed for his car. He had a tip he wanted to follow up on that might put a hole in Troy's alibi. As he reached for the door handle, his cell phone rang. He grabbed the phone from his pocket and answered.

"Hello."

"Luke, this is Dawn from dispatch, there has been a report of a pig loose on the highway. Can you check it out? All cars are occupied."

"I'm sorry, can you say that again?" He pressed his phone against his ear to be sure that he didn't miss a single word. "There is a pig in the middle of the road?"

"Yes, on the highway between Blue River and Broughdon. He might have gotten loose from one of the local farms."

"I'll check it out right now."

"Thanks."

He hung up his phone, then glanced at his watch. He knew that Arnold had an appointment at the vet. Sure there could be many other pigs in the area, but something told him that Arnold might have escaped. As he headed for his car, he dialed Ally's number. It rang several times, then went to voicemail. He left her a message, then tried Charlotte's number. It also rang, then went to voicemail. His instincts began to get riled up. Had they turned their phones off while at the vet? As he got into his car he placed a call to the vet he knew Charlotte used for Arnold. After a few rings, a bubbly receptionist answered.

"Best Vets for Pets, how may I help you?"

"Could you tell me if a pot-bellied pig named Arnold has arrived for his appointment?"

"Are you a family member?"

"No, a friend of the family's." He rolled his eyes at the thought of being a pig's family member. "Could you just tell me if he and Ally made it there for his appointment, please?"

"I'm sorry, sir, I can't give out any patient

information, we have a very strict confidentiality policy."

"Would it make any difference if I told you that I'm a police detective?"

"Do you have a warrant?"

"Really? We're talking about animals here."

"Animals have rights, too, sir. Is there anything else that I can help you with, sir?"

"No, thanks." He hung up and gunned his engine. If it was Arnold in the middle of the road and neither Ally or Charlotte were answering their phones, then there was a very good chance that something was wrong. It didn't take him long to spot the pig, as several cars were beeping and flashing their lights. The traffic flow was too heavy for people to stop. Luke noticed that Arnold seemed to be following a particular vehicle. One glimpse at the name on the side of the van made a cold chill race down along his spine.

"What are you doing following Silvio's delivery van, Arnold?" He recognized the pig right away, both for his size, and his determination. Arnold managed to nearly keep up with the van. It helped that traffic was too heavy for any car to go too fast. Luke pulled up beside the van, and as he suspected Troy was driving. He tried to get Troy's attention. However, Troy just kept his eyes on the road and continued to drive. Luke fell back some, so he could protect Arnold from the other cars. He slid in behind the pig and kept his eye on Arnold. He was clearly getting tired. As he veered off into another lane, Luke followed after him. He managed to follow the pig right to the shoulder of the highway. Arnold went and lay on the ground on the side of the road. His round belly heaved with exhaustion. Luke looked up in time to see the van make a hard turn to catch an exit off the highway. He was torn, as he knew that Charlotte would never forgive him if he left Arnold on the side of the road, but he couldn't let Troy get away. He waved down another car and used his badge to coax the driver out of the car.

"I have backup on the way. I need you to stay

with this pig. Make sure he is safe until another officer gets here. Can you do that?"

The young man nodded, though he appeared to be quite confused. Luke rushed back to his car and took off after the van. As he drove he summoned the help of Dawn from dispatch. He requested Troy's home address, as well as backup. Either Troy was headed for a delivery in Blue River, or his farm. Luke couldn't think of a single good reason that Arnold would be chasing the van unless Ally and Charlotte were inside. He knew if Troy detected he was being followed he might do something drastic. To avoid this he kept several cars away from the van, but never lost sight of it.

***

In the distance Ally heard a siren.

"Mee-Maw, the police!" She hissed her words.

"That could be a good thing, or a bad thing." Charlotte grimaced. "It might cause Troy to panic."

"They're getting closer." Ally leaned up far

enough to peek out through the back window of the van. What she saw took her breath away. Arnold was gone. She searched either side of the road for him, but didn't see him. "Mee-Maw, Arnold has disappeared."

"Do you think he's okay?" Charlotte craned her neck to see out through the window.

"I don't know, I can't see him."

"I hope he's okay." Charlotte's voice quivered.

Just then the van drifted to a complete stop. Ally could see the glow of a red light.

"Now, Mee-Maw, we have to get out now." Ally grabbed her by the elbow and slammed her shoulder against the back door as she pulled the handle. In the same moment that her shoulder connected with the steel of the door the van lurched forward. Charlotte tumbled out of her grasp, and the doors didn't budge.

"Oh no, it's locked." Ally shoved again at the door, but it still wouldn't budge. "Are you okay, Mee-Maw?"

"Yes." Charlotte pushed herself back up on her knees.

"I'm starting to believe there's no way out of here."

"Don't say that. We'll be fine."

"I hope so." Ally gulped as the van went over several bumps. She didn't have to look out the window to know that they had crossed over to the dirt roads on Troy's property. Would the police see that? Would they even care? Or were they just after the pig that was holding up traffic? She peered through the back window and didn't see any flashing lights following after them. Her heart sank. Now the only way out was to somehow escape Troy. She wasn't sure if they would be able to do that on his home territory. He would have the advantage. Her stomach twisted with anxiety. No matter what happened, she knew she had to find them both a way out.

A few minutes later the van stopped again. This time the engine turned off, and Troy stepped outside. Only a few seconds passed before he yanked the side door open.

"Out." He stood beside the door and waited for them to comply.

"If you want us out, you're going to have to come and get us." Ally stood in front of Charlotte. "I know that you're not going to do anything to hurt us while we're inside the van. You wouldn't risk damaging it."

"You don't know anything about me." He chuckled. "I'll do whatever I have to do. That's what sets me apart from the rest of the world. If something is standing in my way, I have no problem obliterating it. Right now, that happens to be you. So do you want to do this the hard way or the easy way?"

"It's okay, Ally." Charlotte placed her hand on her granddaughter's shoulder. "Everything's going to be fine."

Ally frowned as she stepped down out of the van. She turned back to help her grandmother down.

Troy gestured for them to walk ahead of him. He watched them very closely as they began to move.

"Just keep heading straight, I'll tell you when to stop."

Ally bit into her bottom lip to keep from screaming. They were too far away from any neighbors to be heard. She regretted not making more of a scene at Dean's shop. Now that they were isolated on Troy's farm, every last shred of hope she held disappeared. Briefly she thought of Luke, and how he would feel when he discovered what happened. Her heartbeat quickened. It seemed to her that every step she took brought herself and her grandmother that much closer to a terrifying demise. She didn't want to even consider what might happen next, but there was no way to avoid thinking about it.

Charlotte shifted closer to her as they walked and spoke in a whisper. "Ally, we have one advantage."

"What's that?" Ally did her best to keep her

voice just as low.

"Troy doesn't know that we know about the back roads. If we can get into the woods, we can make our way out to the gem shop. It's a risk, because once we make a break for it, he's going to be on top of us."

"I know." Ally grimaced. She was tempted to look back over her shoulder at Troy, but she resisted. Anything that would draw attention to her was a bad idea. "Stay close, Mee-Maw." Ally tightened her grip on her grandmother's hand. She was well aware that Troy had a knife, but if they got far enough ahead of him, they might be able to escape. "On the count of three, we're going." She locked eyes with her grandmother. "Agreed?"

"Agreed." Charlotte nodded as her eyes widened.

"One, two, three!" Ally bolted off, with her grandmother's hand still in her grasp.

Troy's shouts followed after them. He cursed, and threatened, as he tried to catch up with them.

"Keep going, Ally, keep going, I'm okay!" Charlotte managed to keep pace with her as they ran down the road.

Ally was so frightened she could barely draw a breath. Even as her feet struck the dirt road, she felt as if the ground was moving. Her heart raced so much that dizziness swept over her. As they neared the fork in the road, Ally began to think they would really make it out. However, a loud sound behind them, made her stomach drop.

"What was that?" Charlotte looked back over her shoulder. "Oh Ally, run! He's after us on some kind of four wheeler. He's going to catch us!"

"We have to get into the trees. It will be harder for him to catch us there." Ally changed direction from the fork in the road and headed into the trees instead. The roar of the engine haunted her more than any sound ever had. What would Troy do when he caught up? She stepped through some brush and expected her grandmother to be right behind her.

"Ouch!" Charlotte gasped as her ankle rolled

in a small hole hidden by the brush. She grabbed on to a branch to try to keep herself upright.

"Mee-Maw, are you okay?" Ally turned back to look at her.

"I think I've hurt my ankle, Ally. Go ahead, you can get help."

"No way, I'm not going anywhere without you. Here." Ally guided her grandmother's arm over the curve of her shoulder. "We'll just take it a little slower."

"Ally, you should just go." Charlotte tried to put some weight down on her foot, but gasped as pain shot through it. "I don't think I can walk, sweetheart. Please, just go!"

Ally heard the roar of the engine as it drew closer. Her eyes burned with tears as fear sent all of her nerves into high gear. Despite the fear that flooded her she didn't consider for even one second leaving her grandmother behind. Instead, she looked for a place for both of them to hide.

"I'm staying, Mee-Maw. Look, there's some

thicker brush over there. Let's try to hide. Do you think you can make it that far?"

"Yes, I'll make it." Charlotte bit into her bottom lip as bolts of pain rushed through her foot.

Ally helped her over to the brush. It was just high enough that they could hide behind it, and thick enough that she hoped it would obscure them from view. As the engine cut off, Ally's hopes were dashed. Troy obviously had an idea of where they were. She heard footsteps approaching and could barely force a breath into her lungs.

"We need to create some kind of diversion." Charlotte grabbed a handful of pebbles from the sandy soil.

"Wait." Ally placed her hand over her grandmother's closed fist. "I hear something. It sounds like a car."

"Ally, he's almost on top of us." Charlotte crouched down further behind the brush, but as she did her ankle twisted, and the pain that shot through her bubbled up into an unavoidable cry.

She clamped her hand over her mouth, but not in time to muffle it. Troy headed straight for them in the same moment that the roar of an engine tore through the country quiet.

Ally pulled her grandmother's arm over her shoulder and eased her up on her feet. Troy caught her eyes above the brush and smiled. But that smile faded as he was tackled from behind. Ally caught a glimpse of Luke's determined expression as he pinned Troy to the ground.

"Don't move a muscle, or this won't end well." Luke pulled Troy's hands behind his back and handcuffed him.

"Luke, thank goodness you're here." Ally guided her grandmother towards Luke's car. "I think we need an ambulance."

"No, I'll be fine, really." Charlotte waved Luke away.

"Charlotte, what happened?" He gazed at her with concern.

"I just twisted my ankle is all." She tried to

force a smile through the pain.

"Mee-Maw, it's more than a twist." Ally helped her to sit down in the backseat of Luke's car.

"Don't worry, backup is on its way, along with an ambulance."

"How did you find us?" Ally turned to look at him as sirens wailed in the distance.

"Actually, I didn't, Arnold did. I received a report of a pot-bellied pig running down the highway, and I just knew that it had to be Arnold."

"Did you find him? Is he okay?" Charlotte asked frantically.

"Don't worry, he's fine. I found him, he was taking a rest on the side of the road, and I made sure he was safe before I followed after you. I didn't want to spook Troy by bringing too many cars down the back roads at one time. Once I knew he was the one who had you." His voice broke as he stared into Ally's eyes. "I'm just so glad that you're okay, that you're both okay."

"The murder weapon." Charlotte narrowed her eyes. "It's in his pocket. I hope that you can take that right to a judge and get Jeff out of jail."

"I'll do it right after you get that ankle looked at Charlotte." Luke lifted an eyebrow.

"Fine, all right." Charlotte sighed. "But do hurry. I don't want him to be locked up a second longer than he has to."

"Don't worry, Charlotte, I'll make sure he's released."

Ally watched as Troy was loaded into one of the patrol cars. She recalled the first time she'd met him, and how polite he'd seemed.

Charlotte caught sight of the contemplation in Ally's expression. "It's over, sweetheart. Don't dwell on the why or the how, just be glad that it's over."

Ally breathed a sigh of relief and nodded. As another patrol car pulled up she heard a familiar snort. Arnold charged straight for them.

"My hero." Charlotte smiled and reached

down to pat his head. Ally knelt down in front of him and hugged him.

Chapter Sixteen

After a few days of recovery, Charlotte was finally off her crutches, and able to get back in the kitchen.

"Ally, I have the perfect dessert for tonight."

"Mee-Maw, are you sure you're up for baking already?"

"Of course, anything with chocolate is healing, you know that." She winked. "But I think we should make this together. Jeff and Luke are coming for dinner tonight, so we can make it special for them."

"That sounds good to me."

"It's one of my favorite recipes, but I only use it on very special occasions."

"Hmm? And what makes this occasion so special? Might it be Jeff?"

"Shush you." Charlotte grinned. "Get a bowl and a spoon, let's get to work."

By the time Luke and Jeff arrived the entire kitchen smelled of rich chocolate fudge. The scent followed Ally all the way to the front door. She opened it to find Jeff on the other side. She had seen him from a distance, but close-up she noticed his strong presence despite his age. He was a few inches taller than her, with dark black hair that was speckled with gray. She noticed the kindness in his expression.

"Hi Jeff." She smiled at him. "I know we've never had the chance to meet, but I just have to do this." She wrapped her arms around him in a tight hug. "I'm so glad you're here."

"Thank you." Jeff chuckled and hugged her back. "I think we know each other pretty well after all of this, at least the important stuff."

"Yes, you're right about that. Dinner is almost ready."

"Are we having chocolate for dinner?" He grinned. "Not that I'm complaining."

"No, but the smell of our dessert is taking over the whole house."

"I don't mind at all."

Luke stepped in just as Ally started to close the door.

"Hi." He smiled at her and pulled her close for a quick kiss.

"Hi to you, too." She met his eyes with a warm smile. "I hope you're hungry."

"Absolutely."

"Everything is just about ready." She picked up a pile of napkins and silverware to distribute around the table.

Jeff excused himself to greet Charlotte.

Ally set out the last of the silverware and smiled as she caught sight of her grandmother with Jeff. They both blushed, and barely said a word, but the connection between them was palpable.

"Let's eat!" Charlotte directed everyone to the table. "It's so nice that we finally got to do this." She sighed with contentment as she handed a bowl of bread rolls to Jeff.

"Nice for so many reasons." Jeff smiled and accepted the bowl. "I'm surrounded by people who helped to get me out of a terrible situation. I don't think I could be happier than I am right now."

"I'm just sorry it took so long for us to get you out." Luke shook his head.

"No need to apologize for that, Luke. You helped by looking into the murder, and because you did I was able to get out." He looked directly into Luke's eyes. "I am relieved that my name is cleared, and I didn't just get out on a technicality. If I had been released without the real murderer being arrested, there would still be a lot of suspicion hanging over me."

"Troy even admitted to being the one that spray-painted Dean's shop with graffiti. He was trying to take down Dean's business before he even opened it. He didn't want the competition for Silvio. He'd learned about his not so squeaky clean history from Silvio, and had gone after him full force."

"He probably thought he was doing the right thing, since Silvio was the first person to give him a chance," Ally said,

"Maybe he did." Jeff nodded. "It was just bad luck that my mandrel was nearby when the police investigated, and I was there around the time of the murder."

"Hopefully, this can all be put to rest now. I saw Erica at the shop today, and she told me that she put her foot down with Brad and is keeping the shop open. He thought he was going to sell it right out from under her to make a nice profit. The whole time she thought he was handling things, he was actually arranging for someone to buy it. She also said that Silvio was retiring which he has apparently planned to do for a while and now that Troy is going to be in prison he is closing down the shop. So it looks like Dean's shop won't have much competition anymore anyway. When she threatened to divorce Brad, he agreed to transfer the shop into her name." Ally shook her head. "I'll never understand how people can love each other and do that."

"Me neither, but all relationships are different." Charlotte frowned. "I can't believe that Jeff could have spent his life behind bars for something he didn't do."

"The important thing is that Jeff is free and justice was served, even if it was a little late." Luke nodded.

"Just like this dinner." Charlotte laughed as she set lamb chops in the center of the table. "Let's eat!"

Ally settled in a chair close to Luke, and her grandmother sat down beside Jeff. For just a moment, Ally considered just how wonderful it was that they were all together. If things had gone wrong, she and her grandmother might not even be alive, and Jeff might still be behind bars.

"At least we finally got to have dinner together." Charlotte smiled.

As they began to dish food onto their plates, Ally couldn't help but steal glances in her grandmother's direction. She watched as Charlotte spooned mashed potatoes onto Jeff's plate until he laughed and begged her to stop. They certainly did have a chemistry between them that Ally could see sparking every time their hands touched, or their eyes met. As strange as it was to see her grandmother in such a position, it also inspired Ally. Companionship could be found at any age. Their relationship was much stronger than it had ever been.

They were deep in conversation, when the timer on the oven went off.

"Oh, the cakes must be ready." Charlotte clapped her hands as she stood up from the table and headed for the kitchen. Ally followed after her.

"Smells delicious. I wonder how they turned out."

"Looks good." Charlotte peered inside the oven. She grabbed the pot holders and lifted the cakes out of the oven. Right away the kitchen was flooded with a chocolate aroma.

"That smells amazing. I can't wait to taste it."

"Me neither." Luke piped up from the table.

"How did we get so lucky, eh?" Jeff grinned as Charlotte and Ally carried the plates over to the table. She set one down in front of Jeff and then glanced up at him.

"I was going to make a cake like these only bigger so I could bake a file into it, just in case the legal way didn't work out." Charlotte placed a ramekin in front of Jeff.

"Good woman." He grinned at her. "Hopefully, I'll never be in that situation again, but if I am, it's nice to know that you would have my back."

"I will always stand up for the innocent."

"That seems to be a family trait." Luke smiled. "Along with being able to make the best chocolate I've ever tasted."

"You have to eat this cake while it's warm, as it's gooey chocolate cake, and the gooey is the best part. But be careful and blow on it first or it can singe your tongue," Charlotte said.

"Hmm, sweet and sassy just like you." Jeff winked at her.

"Jeffrey!" Charlotte blushed and handed him some ice-cream.

Ally took a deep breath of the delicious scent, and savored being surrounded by wonderful people. As laughter filled the air, she was reminded that she was exactly where she wanted to be and that she was the happiest she had ever been. She noticed Peaches curled up in a chair in the corner of the room and a snort from under the table reminded her that Arnold still had his appetite.

The End

Gooey Chocolate Cake Recipe

Ingredients:

4 ounces semi-sweet chocolate

1/2 cup (1 stick) butter

2 eggs

1 teaspoon vanilla extract

1/4 cup buttermilk

2/3 cup all-purpose flour

1/2 teaspoon baking powder

1/4 teaspoon baking soda

1 tablespoon unsweetened cocoa powder

1/4 cup light brown sugar

4 large or 8 small pieces semi-sweet chocolate

Preparation:

Preheat oven to 325 degrees Fahrenheit. Grease four 6-ounce ramekins with butter. Place the ramekins on a baking tray.

Melt the chocolate and butter together over a low heat preferably in a double boiler. Leave to cool.

Lightly beat the eggs in another bowl. Add the vanilla extract and buttermilk. Mix together.

Pour the cooled chocolate and butter mixture into the egg mixture and mix together.

In another bowl sift the flour, baking powder, baking soda and cocoa. Add in the sugar and mix.

Mix the dry ingredients into the wet ingredients until combined.

Half fill the ramekins with the batter, then place the chocolate pieces in the center of each and cover with the remaining batter.

Place the baking tray with the ramekins into the oven. Bake for 18-20 minutes. Do not overbake because you want the center to be gooey and the chocolate melted.

Remove the ramekins from the oven, let them cool for a minute or two and serve immediately. Raspberries and ice-cream are delicious with these. But you can also serve them with cream.

Enjoy!

More Cozy Mysteries by Cindy Bell

Chocolate Centered Cozy Mysteries

The Sweet Smell of Murder

A Deadly Delicious Delivery

A Bitter Sweet Murder

A Treacherous Tasty Trail

Luscious Pastry at a Lethal Party

Trouble and Treats

Fudge, Films and Felonies

Nuts about Nuts Cozy Mysteries

A Tough Case to Crack

A Seed of Doubt

Macaron Patisserie Cozy Mysteries

Sifting for Suspects

Recipes and Revenge

Sage Gardens Cozy Mysteries

Birthdays Can Be Deadly

Money Can Be Deadly

Trust Can Be Deadly

Ties Can Be Deadly

Rocks Can Be Deadly

Jewelry Can Be Deadly

Numbers Can Be Deadly

Memories Can Be Deadly

Paintings Can Be Deadly

Snow Can Be Deadly

Wendy the Wedding Planner Cozy Mysteries

Matrimony, Money and Murder

Chefs, Ceremonies and Crimes

Knives and Nuptials

Mice, Marriage and Murder

Dune House Cozy Mysteries

Seaside Secrets

Boats and Bad Guys

Treasured History

Hidden Hideaways

Dodgy Dealings

Suspects and Surprises

Heavenly Highland Inn Cozy Mysteries

Murdering the Roses

Dead in the Daisies

Killing the Carnations

Drowning the Daffodils

Suffocating the Sunflowers

Books, Bullets and Blooms

A Deadly Serious Gardening Contest

A Bridal Bouquet and a Body

Bekki the Beautician Cozy Mysteries

Hairspray and Homicide

A Dyed Blonde and a Dead Body

Mascara and Murder

Pageant and Poison

Conditioner and a Corpse

Mistletoe, Makeup and Murder

Hairpin, Hair Dryer and Homicide

Blush, a Bride and a Body

Shampoo and a Stiff

Cosmetics, a Cruise and a Killer

Lipstick, a Long Iron and Lifeless

Camping, Concealer and Criminals

Treated and Dyed

Made in the USA
Lexington, KY
12 May 2017